PRAISE *for* WHYLAH FALLS

"The book stands out, not only for its penetrating depiction of one community, but for the ease with which the author switches between naive romanticism in his poems about young love, through visceral eroticism in depictions of adult relationships, to sharp images of racial oppression and social injustice in poems about violence and despair."

—Verne Clemence, *Saskatoon StarPhoenix*

"One rich vaudeville opera here, folks. Old, lost wherewithals and last summer's garden bronzed: unofficial history, full-blown romance, quiltish narrative, password blues, news clippings, archival photos . . . all toward finding, praising, and preserving 'Beauty.' . . . I'm not exactly sure *what* this book is: a poetic novel, a lyric drama, a receptacle of working-class history, an epic blues ballad, a murder legend, the story of an exile's return, an allegorical appeal on behalf of the last vestiges of beauty in the world? What its structures and textures call to mind are *Paterson*, by William Carlos Williams, and *Coming Through Slaughter*, by Michael Ondaatje. Also Pablo Neruda's meshed images of land and body. I have a sneaking suspicion that *Whylah Falls* might be — dare I say so? — a great book. At least it is fully and marvellously realized. At least I, for one, am humbled by it, am grateful for it."

—Phil Hall, *Books in Canada*

"Clarke is a maximalist. He celebrates the fullness of life and the wealth of our cultural and linguistic traditions. . . . A major delight of *Whylah Falls* . . . is the wide variety of styles Clarke employs: from poet Xavier's imitation of Pound's 'The River Merchant's Wife' to the lyrics of Ma Rainey, from *The Book of Solomon* to a grocer's catalogue, from *The Canterbury Tales* to 'Negro-natural, those green, soiled words/Whose roots mingle with turnip, carrot, and squash,' from journalistic prose to ranting sermon and traditional ballad, all is relished."

—*The Fiddlehead*

"*Whylah Falls* is a cry for identity, joyous and proud and passionate, dazzlingly electric in its incorporation of voices and forms, traditions and perspectives . . . Let *Whylah Falls* have its just adjective: it is gorgeous, in its entirety."

—Mary Dalton, *TickleAce*

"We must, more of us, learn to write like this."

—M. Travis Lane, *Canadian Poetry*

*For a lover of
lavish lyricism!
Warmly,
George Elliott Clarke*

Whylah
Falls

14 août IV

POLESTAR BOOK PUBLISHERS

Whylah Falls

George Elliott Clarke

Polestar Book Publishers acknowledges the ongoing support of The Canada Council;
the British Columbia Ministry of Small Business, Tourism and Culture through the BC Arts Council;
and the Government of Canada through the Book Publishing Industry Development Program (BPIDP).

Design by Val Speidel
Author photo by Daniel Abriel

Many of these pieces appeared in *New Maritimes*, *The Dalhousie Gazette*, *The Dalhousie Review*,
The Antigonish Review, *The Pottersfield Portfolio*, *New Works*, *The Subterranean Times*, *The Idler*,
The Rap, *The Globe & Mail*, *The Toronto Star*, *Imprint*, *The Journal*, *Tickle Ace*, *Germination*,
The Fiddlehead, *The Cormorant*, *Beyond Black Magazine*, *Kola*, *Descant*, *Quarry*, *Caribe*, *Grain*, *Event*,
and *Callaloo* (USA). Others were anthologized in *Poets 88* and *Symbiosis*. And several aired on CBC Radio
(Morningside, Open House, State of the Arts, and Sunday Morning), CKDU Radio (Where Rock Meets Bone),
and on TVOntario (Imprint). "The Apocrypha" poems first appeared in the *Digby Courier*, *Descant*, *left history*
and *Whylah Falls: The Play* (1999). A slightly different version of the "Introduction" was published in
Q1uerry, 40.4 (Fall 1991). Many thanks to the editors and hosts.

Photographs were culled from the Public Archives of Nova Scotia, the National Archives,
and the Author's Archives (*see* page 203).

Canadian Cataloguing in Publication Data

Clarke, George Elliott, 1960–
Whylah Falls

Poems.
ISBN 1-896095-52-6 (bound). — ISBN 1-896095-50-X (pbk.)

I. Title.
PS8555.L3748W49 2000   C811'.54   C99-911322-4
PR9199.3.C5265W49 2000

Library of Congress Catalogue Number:

99-069611 (hardcover)
99-069284 (paperback)

POLESTAR BOOK PUBLISHERS

An imprint of Raincoast Books
9050 Shaughnessy Street
Vancouver, B.C. V6P 6E5
www.raincoast.com

3   4   5   6   7   8   9   10

Printed and bound in Canada.

I know that this traitor language can turn

One truth into another or even

Against itself. Yet, it is all we have.

Cantos

Introduction to the Tenth Anniversary Edition   x

Preface   xxvii

Admission   xxviii

Dramatis Personae   xxix

"Look Homeward, Exile"   xxx

I   The Adoration of Shelley   1

II   The Trial of Saul   31

II   The Witness of Selah   47

IV   The Passion of Pablo and Amarantha   73

V   The Martyrdom of Othello Clemence   99

VI   The Gospel of Reverend F.R. Langford   131

VII   The Adoration of Shelley   159

VIII   The Apocrypha   183

Introduction to the
Tenth Anniversary Edition

How does a miscellany of poems gel into a book? This question is the ground I wish to explore in this informal essay on the origin of my second book of poems, *Whylah Falls*. It took me two years to realize that *Whylah Falls* had become a separate book, and another three years to realize that book. In 1985 I had begun to gather together poems published in various little magazines to justify, following the 1983 release of *Saltwater Spirituals* and *Deeper Blues*, the publication of a second book, a verse collection inspired by assassinations, civil wars, insurrections, and the other blood-stained *bric-à-brac* of our century. The putative manuscript, divided into five sections, was tentatively titled "The Book of Liberty." However, the third section of the manuscript, a group of ten poems, began to expand and separate from the rest of the original manuscript like an amoeba splitting in half. This rogue collection of poems and prose evolved into *Whylah Falls*.

Whylah Falls was born in the blues, the philosophy of the *cry*. Indeed, I was trying to find the emotion of song, to rediscover the Four Muses — Eros, Death, Intellect and Spirit. I attempted to worry the line, each verse line, like a blues guitarist using a piece of glass to alter notes. You see, you have to understand improvisation, how a standard reference can become something else. The text is context for what erupts like a solo — the phrase of iambic pentameter in a strophe of *vers libre*. You have to structure the book like an orchestra, a cordance of brass, woodwind, string, percussion, and other instruments. Against this background, anything can happen. Consider the book as a symphony in which each poem is a passage, sometimes harmonious, sometimes cacophonous. Hence, the narrative emerges from the lyrical — sometimes in counterpoint, at other times in harmony, now merging, now diverging, but always enjoying the liberty of concord and discord.

Whylah Falls was also an attempt to improvise a myth, to honour the era of boxcars stuffed with apples. I wanted to resurrect that lost time when poetry was lightning and rich rain, falling like steel guitar. There was a florilegium of 45 r.p.m. records — three-minute erotic statements I had to treasure, had to treasure, in my poems. In that time, the Liberals wooed southwestern Nova Scotia with flamboyant fiddlers and bottles of political holy water. One dreamer strolled all night under the stars, under the stars. Apple blossoms scudded pink and white. Buchanan plotted an intricate web of patronage. An old woman puffed on a reefer. The manuscript mirrored the history of three churches, steamed clams, fried fish, excessively beautiful women, inhumanely handsome men, dented teapots, linoleum, shotguns, eggs, typewriters, roses, tobacco, Coca-Cola, hydroelectric power, Fournier typeface, full moons, rivers, newspapers, seed catalogues, Nashville and Little Nashville, Mississippi and Montréal. It became a dictionary of innocence and experience.

In truth, I was trying to remember, I was trying to remember, a shy woman's smile and an oval, maple table of unique thickness and sheen. The earth leapt into canyons and lakes while my typewriter tapped hot springs in Banff. There, in 1983, amid sunlight and pines, Richard Lemm and Eli Mandel helped me to retrieve a scarecrow and a crooked kitchen that I had hidden in memory. Suddenly, I could see a radical woman's gifts of coffee, beans, and wieners, her country blues, her blue denim, her pink hair curlers, her white cotton robe, her goldfish, her mathematical intellect, her bluebell-brilliant earth, her tired tractors put out to pasture, her cornbread swelling like sunrise in the night of a pan, her bed swimming with mackerel, her moonshine tasting of sweat and rum and rosewater, her coconut oil pomade, her Bible of roses. I remember strong liquor and strong winds.

An electric storm fell over Edmonton and into my brain. My world was strange: sudden with lyrics. Every line was haunted, every line was haunted, by iambic pentameter. Hence *Whylah Falls* is the Apocalypse — the way the world looks when the Beloved is absent. (In *The Great Code*, Frye states, "The apocalypse is the way the world looks after the ego has disappeared.")

A DEFENCE OF POESY

It could not be otherwise because the poem remembers the quick freshes of its origins in song and in the Eden of the erotic and the morbid. A stubbornly anti-modern artifice, the poem never, never, accepted the twentieth century. It revolted against the Industrial Reaction. Though it altered its diction and its appearance, the poem insisted on recalling Arcadian pastures (every surrealist poem is a hymn to nature) and the history of human passion. Even so, the lyric, be evolving various symbolist, imagist, social realist, and projectivist mutations, was the only poetic form to survive the piggery of capital and the slaughter-house of war.

The poem survives now by gathering unto itself all of the powers of the novel. Indeed, while in Banff, I suffered a profound and effortless vertigo upon reading Gabriel Garcia Marquez's renowned novel, *One Hundred Years of Solitude*.

Anna Knill (née Pietzak) had given me a copy of the book when I had visited her and her husband, Kevin, in Edmonton. Through such epic episodes as the ascension of Remedios the Beauty into Heaven and the tragic fall of the passionate lover Mauricio amid an aurora borealis of yellow butterflies, I learned that myth is the womb of narrative, even poetic narrative. The stories of Garcia Marquez (especially the incredible and sad tale of innocent Erendira, the virgin whored by her grandmother), the novels of Toni Morrison, and the poems of Rita Dove and Michael Ondaatje reinforced that initial revelation.

THE ANXIETY OF INFLUENCE

Shakespeare Herrick Milton Wordsworth
The King James Bible Hopkins Yeats
Pound Eliot Thomas Heaney
Rimbaud Baudelaire Rilke Blake

Basho Li Po Mao Ondaatje
Toomer Césaire Hayden Walcott
Acorn Lorca Ginsberg Marquez
Baraka Dylan Bly and Dove.

In the beginning, it was the epic which conveyed narrative or myth. In fact, the history of poetry up to the Industrial Coup and The War to End All Wars (which dispatched the epic to the ash heap of history) was the production of epopee which unified the values and experience of each linguistic civilization for its own time and for posterity. It was the supreme achievement to which every poet aspired. The canon of great epics is at once a catalogue of great poets: *Beowulf*, Malory's *Morte d'Arthur*, Chaucer's *Canterbury Tales*, Virgil's *Aeneid*, Homer's *Odyssey*, Dante's *Divine Comedy*, Blake's *Jerusalem*, Milton's *Paradise Lost*, Wordsworth's *Prelude*, Goethe's *Faust*, Byron's *Don Juan*, Hardy's *Dynasts*, Jone's *In Parenthesis*, Césaire's *Notebook of a Return to My Native Land*, and others. They exist in virtual isolation in world literature.

But should we lament the passing of epos? Yes, if we cherish the unity of vision, that is to say the faith, which it required to be born. The epic cannot be conceived without a womb of commonly held beliefs. Perhaps the apparent impossibility of epic in our time is akin to the impossibility of the continued existence of Canada as a sovereign state. Perhaps the Canadian is a metaphor for the epic poet. Thus we might join Grant and confess, "We find ourselves like

fish left on the shores of a drying lake. The element
necessary to our existence has passed away."

Although the epic has perished, a memory of its grandeur
and power persists in our era in the extended lyric sequence
— which might even be termed an elegy for the epic.
Pioneered by Dickinson's *Poems*, Whitman's *Leaves of Grass*,
and Baudelaire's *Flowers of Evil*, and furthered by the
modernist masterpieces — Eliot's *Waste Land*, Pound's
Cantos, Hughes's *Fine Clothes to the Jew*, and Williams's
Paterson, the extended lyric sequence has become the major
genre for poets who wish to compose a song for their age.

I had always been fascinated by the epic, having thrice
read *Paradise Lost* and enjoyed Longfellow's *Evangeline*.
On top of this, I fell in love with lyric sequences and other
works that created whole worlds. Dove's *Thomas and Beulah*
(see "Pomade") demonstrated that lyric can limn cosmoses of
human relationships. Jean Toomer used the mixed media
of poetry, prose, song, and play to achieve the same effect
in *Cane*.

TRADITION AND THE INDIVIDUAL TALENT

Thus, when my miscellany of poems written around
an Afro-Canadian village in southwestern Nova Scotia
(or Acadia) began to form into a recognizable whole, an

extended lyric sequence, I possessed a history of the genre to explore. And although the machinery of the epic — the decasyllabic line and iambic meter — had rusted from lack of use, once repaired, it began to find new expression in my verse. Moreover, the encyclopedic tendency of the epic asserted itself. I discovered the poetry secreted in recipes, popular songs, Hansard, newspapers, and the names of flowers, musical forms, even the proper origins of liqueurs. But the epic was always a combination of travelogue, drama, encyclopedia, song, history, and narrative of the ways and means of a particular people. It was a catalogue (a quality which defines the extended lyric sequence as well).

Thus, my manuscript kept changing; it refused to stand still. I would edit it to "completion," when, at once, it would demand a different consciousness, a different landscape of the mind. Writing became an act of layering, of adding and subtracting certain timbres, tones, and tints to permit the better revelation of character, voice, and plot. Even so I had to decide how closely I wanted to reproduce the truths I knew. I opted for a watercolour rather than a photograph, a line-shot rather than a half-tone. I permitted my characters their faults. I chose to write poetry, not sociology.

However, I did attempt to fathom the soul of the village of verse by painting a canvas with black watercolor (bone charcoal), permitting it to dry, and then daubing the bottom border with rainbow pastel flowers that gangled upon luminous green stems. This Creation gleamed under a single loony-sized chalk moon. I saw *Whylah Falls* as an anarchy of flowers, a Nova Scotian *Macondo* or *Twin Peaks*.

I also delivered wrongly jailed words from the prisons of dictionaries, thus liberating popple, *passementerie*, freshes, hyacinthe, glissando, thingabob, lineament, spinny, pottage, *chypre*, serif, Churrigueresque, callaloo, pleasance, sidle, lubricious, upshore, *adreynten*, hullaballo, lindy, diddley, blancmange, sleeveen, canker, gabble, pomade, *chador*, slanty, cuss, sass, nappy, rollick, and rimrack. One new word — *swaft*, a verb meaning "to fall softly" — was minted. I also stumbled upon all those beautiful, abandoned, thematic forms that resembled broken organs, rusted trumpets, warped guitars, yet were still capable of the most unearthly music. Hence, I accepted the alba, the aphorism, the aubade, the ballad, the blues, the chanson, the colophon, the coronach, the distich, the elegy, the envoy, the epistle, the fable, the georgic, the hydrographic, the idyll, the *jeu d'esprit*, the kenning, the lamentatio, the madrigal, the moody, the nominatio, the oration, the plaint, the proem, the querimonic, the rococo, the shanty, the sonnet, the threnody, the unreliable narrator, the vatic, the wondrer, the xxxotic, the yowl, and the zeugma.

I studied the discipline of gossip and yarns, noting that such tales form the matrix of myth. Fragments of true stories were accumulated, sifted, altered, portions discarded, and the remainder transformed into new myth. The fantastic occurs everyday.

Aptly, while I was writing this essay, the *Ottawa Citizen*, a marginal broadsheet, gasped in delight to inform its readers of the tragic-but-true tale of the chainsaw murder of a woman by her husband who then took his own life. While that was indelibly incredible, readers were further astonished to learn that this horror transpired while the couple's teenage daughters were calmly preparing for school. I read this event in the following manner:

> *Weary of split lips, broken noses, black eyes, fractured limbs, and multiple cuts, burns, and bruises — the emblems of his undying love — she took a chainsaw and cut off his head where he lay in bed while the two girls, oblivious, prepared for school downstairs. She had nailed shut the bedroom door and wedged a mattress against it to muffle the sound of the motor and other noises that decency will not allow to be described. Drugged, her husband never knew what happened. He slept into death. Reddened feathers snowed through air.*

Originally, I was shocked by such violence, the ecstasy of gunshots and wounds. I thought it anti-social; then, I realized it is always a profoundly social act. Violence flourishes in every form of narrative, including fairy tales. (McLuhan has observed that "even the frequent sensational absurdity and unreliability of the news cannot annul the total effect, which is to enforce a deep sense of human solidarity.")

If the morbid is one pole of literature, the erotic is the other. Desire transforms reality daily, allowing dream and myth to intrude. I explored films, such as *Desiderio*, with its desert, millennium of rain, and rhythm of desire frustration fulfillment frustration desire, to discover the laws of love. I also savoured the Afro-American, Chinese, French, Japanese, and Spanish experiences of eroticism. Thus, I noted lilies, sunflowers, the transparency of silk, the translucency of cotton, the scent of sandalwood and roses, the taste of cherries and plums, Amaretto and Chartreuse.
I also catalogued the strange peculiarities of shoes, shirts, dresses, pants, robes, socks, nylons, observing the comedic and tragic ways in which they fall in love, even love that costs them their lives as they are ruined by reckless passion. I awakened to the panic of sex and the heart-attack of love.

O had to taste her lips to find out whether they held that same taste of honey. But Layla met his ferocious curiosity not with lips but with the miracle of her skin which was, depending upon the mood of the moonlight, all the colours of the key of C — chocolate, cinnamon, coal, copper. O pelted her body with full kisses, wet kisses. Layla, tall and pure, fell like water, hair spilling back onto the thirsting

bed. Her hips snaked under his, her head moved from side
to side under his kiss, smearing their lips. His hands got
lost in her hair speckled with the sugar from his fingers . . .

While Trudeau was just to argue that the "State has no place
in the bedrooms of the nation," artists do enjoy such liberty
(or, perhaps I should say, responsibility). Love and death are
the two most shocking things that happen to us after birth.

I also learned about paper, silk, cotton, wool, and leather.
I explored design, learning to identify Caslon, Bembo,
Perpetua, Garamond, Janson, Cartier, Electra, Palatino, and
Fournier typefaces. I even learned how to make a good pot
of tea thanks to a recent interview which The Hon. Stanley
Knowles gave *The Hill Times*, a Parliament Hill tabloid. In
it, he revealed that love had inspired his appreciation for the
"leaves". As a lad, Knowles had courted his future bride at
her home where her mother would invariably offer him a cup
of tea which he would invariably decline. One day however,
Knowles relented and discovered that he quite liked the
drink. Here is his recipe for the preparation of tea:

1 *Empty the tea kettle, and fill it with fresh cold water.*
   Boil.
2 *Pour some of the boiling water into the empty teapot.*
   Put the lid on the teapot and let it sit for one minute.
3 *Now, empty the teapot and put it into one or two tea*

bags. Pour in the boiling water (make sure it's still boiling when you pour it in), and fill the teapot. Steep for three minutes.

4 Do not indulge in any shortcuts. Sticking to the rules makes certain that everyone will have a good cup of tea.

(Knowles takes his tea with a spoonful of milk and a spoonful of sugar.)

GENERAL PRINCIPLES OF HARMONY

I also experienced the liberatory phenomenon of African-American song disrupting standard literary discourse like blaring horns. Every poem, attempting to trace the genealogy of love, kept referring, no, deferring to the canon of James Brown, Otis Redding, Aretha Franklin, Diana Ross, Smokey Robinson, Billie Holiday, and Bessie Smith. Their sung literature, that is, *orature*, includes such passionate passages as Robinson's "Fork in the Road" —

If there is something that you don't see eye to eye,
You better think before you tell your love good-bye
Cos your paths may never cross again

— (note his use of iambic hexameter) and Ross's "I'm Giving
You Your Freedom":

> *The price I pay to love you is too much to bear,*
> *And it isn't fair when you don't really care.*
> *I'm giving you your freedom to find somebody new;*
> *There's no sense in the both of us making each other blue.*

The subversive influence of song is such that the mandolin in
Lennon and McCartney's "And I Love Her" can reappear as a
sudden, Spanish mood in a lyric ostensibly written in
Canadian English. Hence, as I confessed earlier, *Whylah Falls*
was born in the blues. Yet, to be more precise, it is a response
to the call of popular angst in radio and folklore. You have to
appreciate call-and-response, the antiphonal impulse. You have
to be able to hear Brown wail and to appropriately respond. I
feel good. Try me. I want you so bad.

I also discovered my oral heritage, namely, the Afro-Nova
Scotian *Africadian* vernacular. After all, speech or rhetoric is
the true base of poetry. Tropology is signification. I sought
to restore the verbal magic of African United Baptist
Association sermons. Shouts, hollers, coos, cries, screams —
the jazz of life — are the music I sought to record. I ain't
jawin': a li'l thoughtful yields the real deal. Words be my
milk and meat for life. Am I lyin'? All I gotta do is stay
black and die.

SEVEN TYPES OF AMBIGUITY

Every word we write is a breath — perhaps our last — against oblivion.

All books are merely delayed dust.

Culture is space and time organized into sensible forms.

Post-modernism is the guilty conscience of modernism.

The lyric sequence is the epitaph of the epic.

Form is as form does.

The child's first cry is the first song.

Make it beautiful.

The secret is to sing.

THE BUSH GARDEN

I discovered so much — that Beauty refuses to be suppressed, insisting on naming itself, that the female characters (who had at first been silent) demanded to be free to critique the unruly romanticism of the males, that elements of history (the Depression, Mussolini, the Maritime Fish Company, Cubism) intrude, that magic realism demands the counterpoint of social realism, that lyric requires episodes of prose, that politics evaporates before aesthetics, that modernism, pursued to its limits, returns to epicity, that myth is the glue of art. The process was one of discovery, a new finding. I needed another language, a fusion of tongues.

Furthermore, the final version of *Whylah Falls* is the memory of what was omitted. Many of the ancestral poems were cannibalized for useful phrases, lines, images which were then resurrected in new pieces. *Many poems are written but few are chosen.*

Finally, *Whylah Falls* was pioneered by friends. They settled it, taming its punctuation, cultivating it plots, planting seeds of idea, and clearing its tangled patches. Without them, this book, this little municipality, would not exist. For instance, they suggested appropriate calibres for the guns, selected certain woods as being best for home-made guitars. They surveyed and mapped every inch of the territory, noting the sudden drops, the quick or slow ascents, the Sixhiboux River, Mount Eulah, Beulah Pines, and St. Mary's Bay. They edited with great passion and precision, setting the boundaries clearly. It was only when the poems, domesticated, formed a community, a village of friends, that *Whylah Falls* was completed. Hence, the cessation of creation was also the cessation of exile. Arriving at the end, the limits of *Whylah Falls*, we knew the place for the first time.

Whylah Falls is a place where the death of poetry has not yet occurred.

DISCOGRAPHY

John Coltrane, *Giant Steps*, Atlantic sd 1311, 1960.

James Brown, *The James Brown Show*, Polydor, jb4 101, 1962.

Portia White, *Think On Me*, White House Records, wh lp 6901, 1969.

Patsy Cline, *Greatest Hits*, MCA, crc mcac 12, 1973.

Supremes, *Baby Love*, Pickwick spc 3383, 1974.

Bob Dylan/The Band, *The Basement Tapes*, Columbia, c2x 33682, 1975.

Ambrosia, *How Much I Feel*, Warner Brothers, wbs 8640, 1978.

Bob Marley, *Kaya*, Island, ilp 9517, 1978.

Georges Bizet, *Carmen*, Capitol-EMI, 4av 34005, 1984.

Sade, *Diamond Life*, CBS, frt 39581, 1985.

Faith Nolan, *Africville*, Multicultural Women in Concert, 1986.

Otis Redding, *The Otis Redding Story*, Vol. 1, Atco, cs 2807, 1986.

The Best of Chess Rhythm & Blues, MCA, chc 6022, 1987.

Blue Rodeo, *Outskirts*, Rique Disque, w4 54718, 1987.

Four the Moment, *We're Still Standing*, JAM, ftm 1987, 1987.

Giacomo Puccini, *Madama Butterfly*, Capitol-EMI, 4xs 36567, 1987.

Miles Davis, *Ballads*, CBS, wct 44151, 1988.

Wynton Marsalis, *The Majesty of the Blues*, CBS, oct 45091, 1989.

Preface to the First Edition

Founded in 1783 by African-American Loyalists seeking Liberty, Justice, and Beauty, Whylah Falls is a village in Jarvis County, Nova Scotia. Wrecked by country blues and warped by constant tears, it is a snowy, northern Mississippi, with blood spattered, not on magnolias, but on pines, lilacs, and wild roses.

> *The beautiful is holiness visible, holiness seen, heard, touched, holiness tasted — "O taste and see how gracious the Lord is" — holiness, smell of Paradise.*
>
> —GILL

> *We see beauty not so much when she languishes in peace, as when she burns in fierce diamond brilliance, forever, hard as steel. And the fire pains, so that we may know the glory of it.*
>
> —BRAGG

Admission

This book was born with the midwifery of Paul Zemokhol, Mary Schmidt, Allan Safarik, Roger McTair, William Knight, Sylvia Hamilton, and John Fraser. However, its sins are mine alone.

Ahab Abdel-Aziz, Steve Heighton, Anna Knill, and Charles R. Saunders were a community of support. Gilbert Daye crafted the music. Howard McCurdy, M.P., permitted hardware access; the Ontario Arts Council provided a vital grant; and the Weymouth Historical Society allowed a splendid kindness.

Julian Ross and Caroline Woodward tended the manuscript with gentle care. They became Muses.

I am grateful to Chan Wai See for her patience and advice. She has made me a more faithful writer.

These poems are fact presented as fiction. There was no other way to tell the truth save to disguise it as a story.

—*George Elliott Clarke*
April MCMXC

Dramatis Personae

Xavier Zachary	*a poet*
Shelley Clemence	*a student and beloved of X*
Amarantha Clemence &	
Selah Clemence	*sisters to Shelley*
Pushkin Clemence &	
Othello Clemence	*brothers to Shelley*
Missy Jarvis	*stepsister to Shelley*
Saul Clemence	*stepfather to, and lover of, Missy*
Cora Clemence	*wife to Saul*
Pablo Gabriel	*a poet, pedlar, and suitor of*
	Amarantha
Jack Thomson	*a politician and rival of Pablo*
S. Scratch Seville	*the murderer of Othello*
Rev. F. R. Langford	*a minister*
Liana Carmel	*a seer*
Lavinia Jarvis	*an anti-seer*
Biter Honey	*a journalist*
Eely	*foe of Langford*

Musicians, Philosophers, Witnesses, Lovers

SCENE: Acadia

Look Homeward, Exile

I can still see that soil crimsoned by butchered
Hog and imbrued with rye, lye, and homely
Spirituals everybody must know,
Still dream of folks who broke or cracked like shale:
Pushkin, who twisted his hands in boxing,
Marrocco, who ran girls like dogs and got stabbed,
Lavinia, her teeth decayed to black stumps,
Her lovemaking still in demand, spitting
Black phlegm — her pension after twenty towns,
And Toof, suckled on anger that no Baptist
Church could contain, who let wrinkled Eely
Seed her moist womb when she was just thirteen.

    And the tyrant sun that reared from barbed-wire
Spewed flame that charred the idiot crops
To Depression, and hurt my granddaddy
To bottle after bottle of sweet death,
His dreams beaten to one, tremendous pulp,
Until his heart seized, choked; his love gave out.
    But Beauty survived, secreted
In freight trains snorting in their pens, in babes
Whose faces were coal-black mirrors, in strange

Strummers who plucked Ghanaian banjos, hummed
Blind blues — precise, ornate, rich needlepoint,
In sermons scorched with sulphur and brimstone,
And in my love's dark, orient skin that smelled
Like orange peels and tasted like rum, good God!
    I remember my Creator in the old ways:
I sit in taverns and stare at my fists;
I knead earth into bread, spell water into wine.
Still, nothing warms my wintry exile — neither
Prayers nor fine love, neither votes nor hard drink:
For nothing heals those saints felled in green beds,
Whose loves are smashed by just one word or glance
Or pain — a screw jammed in thick, straining wood.

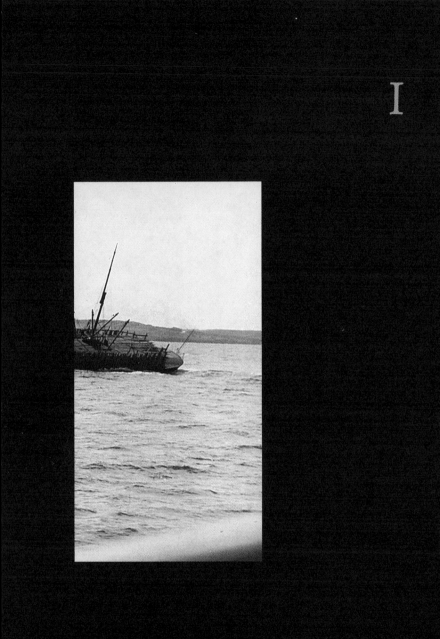

The Adoration of Shelley

I am come into my garden, my sister, my spouse.

— *SONG OF SOLOMON* 5:1

THE ARGUMENT

Crows trumpet indigo dawn. The rose sun blossoms.
A paddlewheel steamer, spilling blues, country, and flamenco
guitar, churns the still Sixhiboux River. Simultaneously, a
dark blue engine steams into Whylah station — a white
marble phantasm. Garbed in baroque motley, a theatre troupe
disembarks. One actor, blurred completely in white,
brandishes an oily shotgun. Another player, a poet, bears a
satchel full of letters and seven books of the elegant verse
that perished in the slaughter of The Great War. His black
suit, tie, shirt, shoes, melt into the dark dawn. A comet
streak of rose flames on one lapel. Thin as any dreamer, this
Mandinga-Mi'kmaq wears circle lenses on his earthen face.
A slow clock, Xavier Zachary turns, his hands crying rose
petals, and wheels upward into the high, blue hills above
Whylah.

Wooooooo! The train howls into steam and vanishes.

Shelley Adah Clemence, eighteen Aprils old, awakens,
stretches in her brass bed. The train moans. She wonders,
"Is this trouble?" Small, slender, she rises, tossing back the
covers like a spurned wave. She resembles Rousseau's
Yadwigha. Same almond-shaped eyes, same sloe-coloured

hair. She peers into her diary, a garden of immortelles and printed sunflowers. Then, Shelley opens her warm Bible and copies verses from The Song of Solomon into her own book. A radio awakens, croons a Ma Rainey song rich with regretful guitars, and Shelley crafts a song with Hebrew lyrics and a Coptic melody:

> *Snow softly, silently, settles*
> *White petals upon white petals.*

She buttons her long, ivory nightdress down to her thin, brown ankles and angles carefully down steep steps to the kitchen, a bath of yellow light. Her ma, Cora, is pulling fire from the woodstove. Othello, her brother, rests his guitar-troubled fingers on a mug of coffee. They suspect that X will arrive shortly, after five years of exile, to court Shelley with words that she will know have been pilfered from literature. Smooth lines come from Castiglione. Shelley vows she'll not be tricked. She be wisdom.

Outside, Whylah shimmers. Sunshine illumines the mirage of literature, how everyone uses words to create a truth he or she can trust and live within.

THE RIVER PILGRIM: A LETTER

At eighteen, I thought the Sixhiboux wept.
Five years younger, you were lush, beautiful
Mystery; your limbs — scrolls of deep water.
Before your home, lost in roses, I swooned,
Drunken in the village of Whylah Falls,
And brought you apple blossoms you refused,
Wanting Hank Snow woodsmoke blues and dried smelts,
Wanting some milljerk's dumb, unlettered love.

That May, freights chimed xylophone tracks that rang
To Montréal. I scribbled postcard odes,
Painted *le fleuve Saint-Laurent comme la Seine* —
Sad watercolours for Negro exiles
In France, and dreamt Paris white with lepers,
Soft cripples who finger pawns under elms,
Drink blurry into young debauchery,
Their glasses clear with Cointreau, rain, and tears.

You hung the moon backwards, crooned crooked poems
That no voice could straighten, not even O
Who stroked guitars because he was going
To die with a bullet through his stomach.
Innocent, you curled among notes — petals

That scaled glissando from windows agape,
And remained in southwest Nova Scotia,
While I drifted, sad and tired, in the east.

I have been gone four springs. This April, pale
Apple blossoms blizzard. The garden flutes
E-flats of lilacs, *G*-sharps of lilies.
Too many years, too many years, are past . . .

Past the marble and pale flowers of Paris,
Past the broken, Cubist guitars of Arles,
Shelley, I am coming down through the narrows
Of the Sixhiboux River. I will write
Beforehand. Please, please come out to meet me
        As far as Beulah Beach.

TO X

Dear X:

You asked how I'm doing. I take the D.A.R. train up the line
to Jarvis once a month; and I study the woman wisdom hidden
in letters, diaries, and songs. One thing I've found is the
chastity of numbers. Take the number nine. It mirrors any
number to which it's wed. Here's the sum of my argument:

$9+7=16=1+6=7$

The same miracle happens with multiples of nine:

$18+16=1+8+1+6=9+7=16=1+6=7$

or $18+16=34=3+4=7$

Numbers reveal truth. Words always have something to hide.

Remember Rafael Rivers who works at the up-and-down
mill in New France, back by the Seven Pence Ha' Penny
River? He doesn't know books but he knows good jokes.
We go out some.

I'm leaving in June to work all summer on the Yarmouth-
Boston steamers. I'm hoping to scrounge enough for
teachers's college next year.

Me and ma and all are glad you're coming down.
It's spring!

Bessie Bird flits from limb to limb.
Apple blossoms petal the snow.

Watch out for living gales. God speed.
Shelley

Othello staggered in the yard, he lurched,
Squared his fist in my face, and spat, "If you
So much as dream that you and my sis' might . . ."
That night was moist with chance, the liquid shock
Of lightning. The river crashed like timber.
Tarpaper homes collapsed under the weight
Of scarlet Liberal election lies.
    You fed me coffee, weiners, beans, and bread;
I wept love poems with tragic majesty,
Remembering every epic failure,
The cigarette smoke of café Marxists,
The pearl of moon above the pawnshop's pearls,
When I staggered across the spine of Montréal,
From Pie IX to Berri-de-Montigny,
In dark loneliness and indigo lust.
Five years later, Shelley, I can't forget.
We are our pasts. Nothing is forgotten.

ROSE VINEGAR

In his indefatigable delirium of love, Xavier wires rugosa rose blossoms to Shelley. Deluded by his quixotic romanticism, he cannot yet appreciate the practical necessities of friendship. But, Shelley trusts in reason; thus, though she admires the blossoms for their truthfulness to themselves, she does not hesitate to distill a delicate and immortal vinegar from what she considers the ephemeral petals of X's desire. An ornament becomes an investment. She fills a cup with the fresh rose petals; then, stripping off their heels (the white part), she pours the petals into a quart sealer and adds two cups of white vinegar. Then, she seals the jar and places it on the sunny livingroom windowsill for sixteen days, seven hours, and nine minutes. When the vinegar is ready, she strains it through a sieve and then pours it back into the bottle.

Rose vinegar. It's especially good on salads.

BEES' WINGS

This washed-out morning, April rain descants,
Weeps over gravity, the broken bones
Of gravel and graveyards, and Cora puts
Away gold dandelions to sugar
And skew into gold wine, then discloses
That Pablo gutted his engine last night
Speeding to Beulah Beach under a moon
As pocked and yellowed as aged newsprint.
Now, Othello, famed guitarist, heated
By rain-clear rum, voices transparent notes
Of sad, anonymous heroes who hooked
Mackerel and slept in love-pried-open thighs
And gave out booze in vain crusades to end
Twenty centuries of Christianity.

His voice is simple, sung air: without notes,
There's nothing. His unknown, imminent death
(The feel of iambs ending as trochees
In a slow, decasyllabic death-waltz;
His vertebrae trellised on his stripped spine
Like a xylophone or keyboard of nerves)
Will also be nothing: the sun pours gold

Upon Shelley, his sis', light as bees' wings,
Who roams a garden spring from rotten wood
And words, picking green nouns and fresh, bright verbs,
For there's nothing I will not force language
To do to make us one — whether water
Hurts like whisky or the sun burns like oil
Or love declines to weathered names on stone.

SPRINGTIME AND THE LIVING

A butterfly, fuzzed rainbow, emerges from its chrysalis. Shelley awakes to sunlight. She unpins her hyacinthine hair, the living-groom fills with scents of bergamot and peach. Her skin is gold leaf; her bones — illuminated scrolls. Her face shimmers with a light as diffuse as that glimpsed through bees' wings.

Dumbfounded, I return to the bland expectancy of pages, while Othello, curled on the couch, grumbles, conjures fresh blues from stale beer. Cora bustles into the dawn, hollers, "Lower the blind! I can't see! Everything's too bright! Has the Apocalypse come early?" While she tugs the vanilla-flavoured blind, a timber truck lumbers past, loaded with raw news and unprocessed love letters still locked in bark and leaves.

I sneak a glance at Shelley. She smiles and reaches for the dented teapot. Does she spy Casanova or Romeo behind my smile? Peeking outside, I watch three crows flicker past like black lightning or winged premonitions taking the shortest route between two prophecies.

The next thing we know, three Thessalonians bust through the door, babbling about a freak thundershower and bothering the goldfish in their globe of water. Scattering fresh rain, Pablo, the first, spits out a country song full of pits and thorns. He gets so loud that Cora stuffs his mouth deliberately with a conspiracy of coffee and toast. Amarantha, the second, laughs in the lop-sided kitchen, quaking the floor. She hugs herself as if cold or lonely, and Cora baptizes her with a quilt. Pushkin, the third, sits by the iron woodstove and ruminates over an open guitar about an unhealed hurt that he suffered a century ago. He begins with a mouthful of Bible and ends with a home-made proberb: "History tends everything."

Now that the house is so busy, I get up, with all my poems and secret loneliness, and walk outside. God has unpeeled a rainbow above the house. In the garden, flowers gangle, tangle with squash, cucumber, sweet potato, lumber. I spy the carpen-try of branches nailed to a pale blue sky, and craft several, invisible prayers just to persuade Shelley to come out her door. Then, she emeges and looks my way. In a notebook, I ink, quickly before she can see, a negroid haiku:

> I got a gal, sweet as sweet can be:
> She walk through thunderin' rain, just to be with me.

The whole time I fear that Shelley'll discover my lovin' lyrics and bar me as a lunatic when I'm just a Romantic fool in the wrong century for adoration. But Shelley says nothing. She just stares at the roses. I retreat to her house to try to conjure the nerve to deliver a fresh ultimatum of love.

Groggy, Othello sits up, draws himself into a Buddha pose. He seems half-asleep. Suddenly, he jumps as if ice has plopped into his lap, but it's just Pablo, sliding Pushkin's acoustic guitar — an abandoned child — across his thin thighs. Othello picks it up, cradles it, and coos, filling that strung wood with a separate life. He tickles it to see how sensitive it is. Then, he caresses it, and lonesome for its mother, some splintered pine, it begins to cry. Slowly, Othello nurses it from its blues and it gets to gigglin' in a fit of "Froggy Gone Courtin'," its strings smilin'.

Yellow butterflies waft from the stove, Pushkin stands and jigs, resembling the query-shaped scarecrow that Langford has rigged to his roof, the goldfish jiggle, Pablo patches together a crazy quilt canticle fofr Am, his intended, the once and future Scallop Queen of Jarvis County. And now, too, I know I love Shelley hopelessly, no matter whether Cora approves or whether O breaks my bones to preserve his sister from my poems.

Othello and Pablo meld voices and make music reminiscent of the United Soul Kingdom guitarists who milk velvety blues from discontented chords. I wander outdoors again, watch crows flicker overhead like theoretical algebra.

> *Blackberry, blackberry, on the vine,*
> *Sweet, bittersweet, blackberry wine,*
> *When will you be mine, all mine?*
> *When will you be mine?*

15

HOW EXILE MELTS
TO ONE HUNDRED ROSES

I climb to Whylah Falls because I thirst,
Hunger, for you, Shelley, and shake to touch
Your house that slides down Mount Eulah to fog —
The misery of the Sixhiboux River.
My five-winter exile now melts
To roses gorged where tears once hammered dirt.

   I dream the poems I sent all smell of grass
And gold daisies sprouted in a tumbler,
While song cartwheels in air scrubbed deaf to threats
Of disaster, and fiddle-eights cry out
With crows, wedding memory with desire,
And I peer through pined distance to your home:
Pushkin drawls dirty songs, his banjo packed
With bluebells and mayflowers; plump Cora whoops,
Cackles, tells him to "Keep a-strummin', man!"
Othello looses pants, spills into bed
With Liana, and their feet never touch
The floor until morning. Pushkin's voice twangs,
Then, smelling of plug tobacco, and staggered
By home-stilled rum, he winks out in Cora's lap.

   I ramble home and find love's fleshed: mermaids

And drunk sailors kiss in the Sixhiboux;
Bearded, black saints, reeking of oil, comb fields
That plunge to poverty to budget soothes;
Revered Langford hollers against silk
And money, devil booze and bingo chips,
And false communion between the sexes,
Then slinks to Liana once O is done.
Mrs. Belle Brooks gulps marijuana smoke,
Uncorks seventy-five years of gossip,
To preach scotch-breathed sermons of tinfoil-winged
Angels hauled from pines or pulled, naked,
From sties. Shelley, we wrest diamonds from coal,
Scrounge pearls from grubs and stones, lest penury
Work filthy rags of our magnificence,
Or planners bulldoze our flowers into dirt.

   I love you, Sweets — your eyes black with sorrow,
Your Sphinx-like smile, your breasts like ripe apples!
I hurry home, weary of seeking love
In banks and trusts, lusting to clench you tight —
While night is wet with fire, the earthy taste
Of mushrooms black with dew, the ash of figs —
And sweat love until crows usher in dawn.
Shelley, I pick my steps out of the earth!

HOW EXILE MELTS
TO ONE HUNDRED ROSES:
POSTSCIPT

All my miles have melted to this song of how the brown girl
— Shelley — squirrels away, in her bureau, a hundred
postcards proclaiming her beautiful, although she's been
schooled that her hotcombs and dented teapot and black
woodstove are backward, backwoods, and unbecoming. But I
love her bluebell-brilliant earth, her tired tractors put out to
pasture, her cornbread — sunrise swelling in the night of a
pan, her bed swimming with mackerel, her moonshine tasting
of sweat and rum and rosewater, her coconut oil pomade . . .

And all my poems have sprouted into this gold daisy, this
memory, of how, at the slightest touch, Whylah Falls sunlight
turns to rain, how the Sixhiboux River, rusted by stones and
sewage, pours brown into the blue bay, and how Shelley
rouges her lips 'til they gleam glad like God sayin' she is His
wife in whom He is well-pleased.

THE LOVER'S ARGUMENT
WITH SHELLEY

Shelley, I climbed to Whylah Falls while dusk
Scattered elm and crow shadows across your crooked
Kitchen. Now, I knock on your door and lean
Inside, looking for you. Shy, scared, you twist
Away, look out your twisted window,
And stare at black opacity.

   You remember a floundered lumber truck,
That heaviness that hooked Rafael's breath,
Ripped it from his stunned lungs, when his truck leapt,
Reeled, flopped, on Whylah's sharpest hill.
Gravity set his corpse awry, crooked,
Like a Picasso trick, and grave-dirt blackened
Your small, brown hands. Now, love's lies.

                      But, Shelley,
My love is plain; I've stripped bark from pencils,
And stoked your stove with pamphlets and old news.
My poems, thrown to the creek, gleam, wriggle, leap.

Shelley, the moon gapes, refuses to go away.
Let us go down by the bright Sixhiboux
And sit where thingabob uncorked his voice
And elders baptized him in snow-white robes.
Let us catch, unawares, some trout, some sleep.
Shelley, the end of this world is Beauty.

THE STUDENT'S TALE

Everyone cries for love —
but here's the truth of love:

There was no struggle —
just Uncle Cle uncoiling through the door.

He did three murders —
even their son, wound in her womb.

Aunt Io ruined — a bullet
huddled in her skull.

Pardon my doubts
and my grammar.

But don't *l'amour*
echo *la mort?*

BLANK SONNET

The air smells of rhubarb, occasional
Roses, or first birth of blossoms, a fresh,
Undulant hurt, so body snaps and curls
Like flower. I step through snow as thin as script,
Watch white stars spin dizzy as drunks, and yearn
To sleep beneath a patchwork quilt of rum,
I want the slow, sure collapse of language
Washed out by alcohol. Lovely Shelley,
I have no use for measured, cadenced verse
If you won't read. Icarus-like, I'll fall
Against this page of snow, tumble blackly
Across vision to drown in the white sea
That closes every poem — the white reverse
That cancels the blackness of each image.

THE WISDOM OF SHELLEY

You come down, after
five winters, X,
bristlin' with roses
and words words words,
brazen as brass.
Like a late blizzard,
You bust in our door,
talkin' April and snow and rain,
litterin' the table
with poems —
as if we could trust them!

I can't.
I heard pa tell ma
how much and much he
loved loved loved her
and I saw his fist
fall so gracefully
against her cheek,
she swooned.

Roses
got thorns.
And words
do lie.

I've seen love
die.

EACH MOMENT IS MAGNIFICENT

Othello practices *White Rum*, his scale of just music, and clears the love song of muddying his morals. He sets his glass down lovingly, a whole chorus of molecules sloshing in harmony. He vows he will not, he will not be a dead hero, no way, suffering a beautiful sleep, trimmed with ochre, hazelnut, dressed in mahogany, smelling of last-minute honey and tears, regrets rained upon him too late in the guise of wilted, frail flowers. Instead, he will sleep right now, while he still can, up to his thighs in thighs, gnaw dried, salty smelts, and water song with rum. *Sweet Sixhiboux, run softly till I end my song.*

Wearing the lineaments of ungratified desire, Selah sashays from the livingroom, watches dusk bask in the River Sixhiboux. She tells Othello to shut up because Jericho's where she's gonna go when she falls in love. Yep, when that someday man come out the blue to Whylah Falls, Beauty Town, to serenade her and close his wings around her, she'll be in Jericho at last like the fortune-teller says. She'll jump the broom and cross the Nile.

I stroll outside with strange music in my skull. Here's the Sixhiboux River, tossed tinfoil, crinkling along the ground, undistracted by all the grave lovers it attracts, all those late Romantics who spout Lake Poet Wordsworth, "The world is too much with us, late and soon," and brood upon the river's shimmering bliss before tossing themselves within, pretending to be Percy Bysshe Shelley at Lerici. I've thought of the Sixhiboux in those erotic ways, dreamt it as being midnight-thick, voluptuous, folding — like a million moths, furry with a dry raininess — over one. No matter where you are in Sunflower County, you can hear it pooling, milling in a rainstorm, or thundering over a hapless town. Even now, I can hear its shining roar pouring over Shelley's house, polishing the roses that nod, drunken, or spring — petalled crude — from earth. All I hear is an old song, her voice, lilting, "Lover Man."

She's absent, far from here. My blood moves angry through its rooms; rain washes all my tears to the sea. My pain will never end unless I can sleep beside my love, pluck the ripe moon, halve it, and share its sweet milk between us: *Hear me, oh moon, hear my song:*

> *I am like that road that slinks to your door*
> *Like a married lover, sneaking around*
> *To curve his ribaldry about your form.*
> *Shelley, that's how much, that's how much, I feel.*

SOLITUDE

A gull drops to kiss
   its dark, watery double,
      soars again alone.

TO THE READER

He sang all night under the moon
For dreamers yet to love, who might
Find his lyrics some star-dark night,
And be themselves singer or sung.

II

The Trial of Saul

My soul has grown deep like the rivers.

— HUGHES

THE ARGUMENT

Saul Clemence. May God have mercy on his soul. His love
has become a series of effortless mistakes. He aged a labourer
in a century that hates work. He spent all he is gouging
gypsum from a hillside, so his lungs are silver-coated with
sickness and his heart dries now to bone and his conscience
is rusted metal. Who dast blame this man if he makes his
stepdaughter his lover and his wife his foe? Yet, jury of
readers, there is no defence for these social crimes. These
sins are Mr. Clemence's own. True, he has been sinned
against: fifty years is too long to spend, a hunchback, stooped
in a damp, vicious cave, dark with smoke and tuberculosis,
shovelling gypsum just for the pennies to fix one's shoes. So
folks, our hands are dirty. As surely as iodine or gypsum
dust, we've helped to poison him. But it's too late for our
tears. Besides, he is tired of hope. His nerves are calloused.
He has shovelled his life away like gypsum.

So, study his face as lined as the page of a book. Feel his
hands: rough gloves that heft gypsum and do easy harm. He
resembles our dream of Samson. His speech is gravel.

The curtain parts to reveal the interior of a modest,
hidden home. Mississippi John Hurt pries "Black Snake

Blues" from the first radio. Old Saul Clemence appears, lying in a disturbed bed beside his young stepdaughter Missy Jarvis. Having abandoned Cora — his wife and her mother — years before, he sits up in a panic. The radio shifts abruptly into anything by Billie Holiday.

X discovered this florilegium of bad love encoded in five years's worth of Shelley's elegant epistles that he carried in his satchel alongwith volumes of verse by Hardy, Bridges, Roberts, Carman, Johnson, Dunbar, and Yeats. With Shelley exiled, he began to realize the fragility of desire.

HOW TO LIVE IN THE GARDEN

And the Lord God took the man, and put him into
the garden of Eden to dress it and to keep it.

—GEN. 2:15

Cora brings a rural nobility to making food, a solid love,
staring into her huge, copper pot like a gardener staring into
a pot of lush earth, bright soil, glistening with newness, or
tending a *bonsai* tree, the trunk of steam rooted in the
pottage, the branches of steam wafting into nothingness. She
salts her stored, miniature sea, churns it with a walnut spoon,
then lifts goodness, a kiss, to her lips while spicy, flamboyant
smells green her kitchen into Eden.

Cooking is faith. Cora opens her antique cookbook, a
private bible, enumerating Imperial measures, English orders,
— pinches, pecks, cups, teaspoons, of this or that — and
intones, "I create not food but love. The table is a
community. Plates are round rooves; glasses, iced trees;
cutlery, silver streams."

Her Jarvis County cuisine, gumboing the salty recipes of
Fundy Acadians, the starchy diets of South Shore Loyalists,
and the fishy tastes of Coloured Refugees, includes rappie

pie, sweet potato pie, pollen pancakes, steamed fiddleheads, baked cabbage, fried clams, dandelion beer, mackerel boiled in vinegar, and basic black-and-blue berries. For breakfast, Cora offers fried eggs, sausages, orange marmalade, and toast, washed down with rich coffee. Her tastes are eccentric, exotic, eclectic. Her carrot cake consists of whole carrots whose green, leafy tops sprout from brown, earthen icing and whose orange roots taper to the cake's floor. She bakes apple tree leaves, blossoms, seeds, and bark into her apple pies. Cora is the concrete poet of food.

This afternoon, she thawed a pound of cod filets, white flesh raw but succulent on the plate, and diced it into one-inch squares. Then, she sautéed a half cup of sliced onions in rich, yellow butter and poured the sizzling aroma into a broth made from celery soup, a cup of water, and a cup of milk. Next, she stirred the mix and added the fish, Jarvis scallops, and Church Point clams, nursing the chowder to a boil. Cora simmered it for seven minutes, then sprinkled the smiling sea with chopped parsley. *Voilà!* Perfection under gravity . . .

Cora's dandelion wine is a great agony of sunflowers. No, dandelions. It must be drunk to be believed. (One believes it when drunk.) It tastes like Russian literature, sunlight shining through birch leaves. It curls into a glass, snarls along the sides and bottom, doubling, tripling, quadrupling upon itself. (Watch the white curl of cream churn into clear, brown tea, touch bottom, then billow along the sides and up, muddying the water.)

THE SYMPOSIUM

Don't gimme nothin' to jaw about, Missy, and I won't have
nothin' to holler for! Just sit back, relax, and be black. I'm
gonna learn you 'bout the mens so you can 'scape the bitter
foolishness I've suffered. A little thoughtful can save you
trouble.

Missy, you gotta lie to get a good man. And after you gets
him, you gotta be set to hurt him to hold him, so help my
Chucky! 'Cos if you don't or won't or can't, you're gonna be
stepped on, pushed 'round, walked out on, beat up on,
cheated on, worked like a black fool, and cast out your own
house.

Don't suck your teeth and cut your eyes at me! I be
finished in a hot second. But you'll hear this gospel truth so
long you, my oldest, eat and sleep in my house. Best cut
your sass!

Pack a spare suitcase, one for him. If he proves a lucifer, it
be easier to toss him out that way. Put one change of clothes
into it so he can't beg and bug you for nothin'!

If he be too quiet, he'll ruminate and feel that bottle more
than he will you. Rum'll be his milk and meat for months.
It'll spoil him for anything. Won't be fit to drive his nail no

mo'. So when he's sleepy drunk, smack the long-ass son of a gun in the head, tell him to wake his black-ass body up, and drive him out. If the fair fool don't come back sober, he don't come back. Am I lyin'?

And if he be sweet-lookin', a heavy-natured man, always pullin' on women, and he takes up with some spinny woman all daddlied up from the cash he's vowed to bring you, just tell him right up and down that you ain't his monkey in a dress, and raise particular devil. Don't give him no shakes. And if that don't work, don't waste another black word. Grab yourself a second man.

Watch out for two-faced chroniclers. These women will grin in your face, lookin' for news 'bout you and your man. And just when you trust their trashy talk and make your man groan and grump and get all upset, these gold-dust whores creep behind your back, crawl right in your bed, and thief him away. That's how they act. I know: I've been gypped so bloody much. And they don't care if it's a used love, a second-hand love, a stolen love, 'cos it's love all the same. And if it's good to you, they'll try to trick some too. So don't put no business on the streets that's conducted 'tween your sheets. But if some big-mouth humbugs you, tell the black bitch not to mess 'cos she's terrible lookin' anyway; a knife gash 'cross her face would just be improvement.

Missy! Gimme some of that bottle! Preachin' parches the throat. Besides, my eyes feel kinda zigzaggy today.

If some woman is grinnin' at your man, tell her straight:
"If it was shit that I had, you'd want some of that too."
Make her skedaddle. If her fresh fool follows, take
everything he got and don't give a single, black penny back!

Missy, life's nothin' but guts, muscle, nerve. All you gotta
do is stay black and die.

THE CONFESSION OF SAUL

Foot was killin' me.

Ripped off the bleedin' shoe;
the friggin' spike
had drove clean through.

Pain was
fire, salt,
needles,
sour water.

A good daughter,
Missy come,
comfortin', tender,
bound my tore foot
with her shirt.

She ripped her shirt
and I eye
her maple treats.

That
was that.

My love come down
like sweet water.

THE SEPARATION

Saul bawls at his wife, shouts damnation,
Hulks at the summit of the tumbling steps
And hauls fresh fire right out of the air.
Cora shrieks, cringes by the steep stairs
That flee into the dark, bottomless hall.
The roof heaves with the rush of wings; the house
Shudders for Saul's heavy fists pummel walls.
Purposely uneyed, he seizes darkness,
Curses thirty damned years of marriage,
And hoists Cora's cedar chest into air —
And dashes its soft brains upon the stairs.
Jewellery trembles, coins panic, clothes flinch.
Splinters and ramifications escape,
Riot in air, like Pandora's troubles.
Cora screams for love but she screams in vain:
How can Saul hear *Creation's* groans?

CORA'S TESTAMENT

Mean-minded Saul Clemence, ugly as sin,
Once pounded, punched, and kicked me 'cross the floor;
Once flung me through the second-storey glass:
My back ain't been right for clear, twenty year.
But I bore it, stuck it out, stood his fists.
He be worms now. How'd I take up with him?

   Uncle was sniffin' me, and I'd be damned
If I 'lowed him to stir my sugar bowl,
And I shushed a cryin' doll; so when skirt-
Crazed Saul, who trudged nine miles and back to pitch
Gypsum, come courtin' me, I swept his house,
Slept in his bed.

      Why he always beat me?
I was too jolly scared to run around.
I was true to him like stars in the sky.

43

A PERSPECTIVE OF SAUL

Washed out by whisky, Saul slouches and pules
goddamn Nova Scotia mean 'Pression blues
quick as the joy jars and hope weed are gone.
He don't seem to 'preciate that fields
can't bloom with blossoms
forever and forever and forever.

    He stinks of dime-store cologne.
His hands are mistaken with the hammer:
nails bumble and break before driven.
He's too old to be loved forever.

    I ain't ma.
I'm gonna wind away like the wind.

THE POISONING

Scatting, in a voice cold as winter wind
Over corn, nails hammering wood across
Windows, that his quilt is too worn for warmth,
That she's in cahoots for Weymouth this moon,
With her hotcomb and six-foot-strong Eely,
Missy 'mits, "I don't love ya no mo'," and
Blue-black night pummels Saul's eyes with hard shade.
His huge hands wrestle with slippery prayer.
    The door groans shut. Missy's Ford moans. Saul slips
To tremors, tears, the hurt of brandy, sips
Iodine, a brew sharpened like acid,
Until his speech corrodes, blackens, to slurs,
Drooled gasps, drawls, of lover runnin' lover,
Until dumb desire froths white at his mouth
And he ceases amid kindling and cold
With no reason or good-bye for Missy,
Only the openness of eyes after
A final lunge at light, only gossip
Passed like proverbs, grey folks wagging their heads,
Crying, "All that for a black girl!"

III

The Witness of Selah

You never get nothing
By being an angel child . . .
Wild women don't worry,
Wild women don't have the blues.

—COX

THE ARGUMENT

Stars are bread crumbs. Selah Clemence wonders, "Is this all
there is?" She stumbles, in a delicate drunk, a green path.
The moon fidgets like a maniac. When she finds her
bedroom, she places pine branches in her dresser to perfume
her clothes that otherwise would smell of roses. Pablo
Gabriel calls her "Gatito," Spanish for "little cat." She is that
lithe. Queen Natchal. How could she be otherwise? She
stages a pageant of colours — silver, crimson, and yellow —
against the backdrop of her dark skin.

She soaks in bright scents of *chypre*, coconut, and honey
so that she is consciously sweet. She indulges in such
extravagant gestures as her hands nonchalantly stroking her
voluptuous hair and other Romantic acts such as draping her
red silk panties on the edge of a bathtub where a choice
explorer can find them. A brash innocent, always she is dying
for love of some no-count man who abandons her always
after a month of epic scandals that forever brand him a
bastard and the most miserable dog in Jarvis County.

She is a modern martyr for love, bearing witness to its
betrayal by men who fear their own nakedness. Thus, she has
made alcohol her one true love. She has wedded liquor

because men have betrayed her sexuality as they have betrayed their own. Public songs stolen from crackling radios, warped records, and tavern performances are her refuge, her dowry, her diary of hurt, her modernism, her lyric beauty already become tragic although she is only twenty-nine. When a camera squints upon her, it x-rays her flesh, discovering keyboards, guitar strings, and flute holes hidden in her bones. Selah is Beauty oppressed because of its perfection. She quotes Bessie Smith:

> You can't trust nobody,
> You might as well be alone;
> Found my lost friend,
> And might as well stayed at home.

Because Shelley is absent, X — a bee hunting nectar — stumbles upon Selah. When he kisses her, her clothes dissolve like cotton candy. In the beginning, their love is artless, a duet between acoustic guitar and saxophone. Later, it is the ugly sound of innumerable bottles of Scotch and rum and beer being incessantly filled and emptied in the basement of the twentieth century. Oh, reader, our lives are the tombs we build around ourselves.

KING BEE BLUES

I'm an ol' king bee, honey,
Buzzin' from flower to flower.
I'm an ol' king bee, sweets,
Hummin' from flower to flower.
Women got good pollen;
I get some every hour.

There's Lily in the valley
And sweet honeysuckle Rose too;
There's Lily in the valley
And sweet honeysuckle Rose too.
And there's pretty black-eyed Susan,
Perfect as the night is blue.

You don't have to trust
A single, black word I say.
You don't have to trust
A single, black word I say.
But don't be surprised
If I sting your flower today.

BRINGING IT ALL BACK HOME

I

The Jarvis County moon has turned up as gold as Selah's Selassian vision of Africa. Pleased, Selah reclines, making soap go crazy in the tub. She thinks luxury is what the Twenties were about and she don't care who disagrees. Later, extracted and rubbed down, she moans into her diary, "I'll never be, I'll never be, I'll never be marrried." She dreams herself laced lusciously in white, her dark breasts coddled by white silk as if they were delicately wrapped *bonbons* or two verses from The Song of Solomon. Uncannily, that's the very song taken up by Pablo, who desires a woman with a belly heaped with wheat and set about with lilies. But he doesn't see Selah, only Amarantha, her navel — a round goblet which wanteth not liquor.

"I am my beloved's, and his desire is towards me," Selah sings, but Pablo is deaf. He smokes love song cigarettes rolled from Ellington tobacco and dipped in Rainey sorrow. Each cigarette contains 78 r.p.m. of pain per love affair: He knows he'll die of a cancered heart. He puffs and groans:

I'm movin down that soft road
To part your warm, warm river.
I'm gonna plunge in deep
'Til I start to shiver.
Then I'm gonna wade back in,
Make your water quiver.

11

Far beyond the kitchen door, Amarantha teeters up and down the road, reeling as if she's aboard a ship, feeling the earth roll beneath her feet because of excessive love and too much alcohol. She slips precipitously and sinks up to her delicate thighs in asphalt and dirt and bad sex. When she looks up, she gets angry: *Why won't one of those goddamn, stuck-up stars reach down a warm hand and help her up?*

In that Sargasso of gravity, Am recalls that one night, Pushkin was discovered shamefully dead drunk, half-sunken in the road, and had to be pretzeled into the back of a car and then tucked into his front door. When Selah opened it, he collided with the floor. Then, because it was in his way, he tore up the carpet and smashed through floorboards, splintering his fist and screaming into black emptiness, "Lemme out! Lemme out!" Ma had come running, lifted him sideways, and buried him in a bed that was as warm

and white as his most exotic memory of his best white
woman.

III

Crying, "Return O Shulamite; return, that I may look upon
thee," Pablo abandons Cora's to seek Am. He cuts his car
engine on the evil road that, tearing into rocks and trees,
veers away from man to become *Terror*, a writhing being who
slithers steeply into turns, tipping timber trucks or flinging
flivvers into solid space. When Pablo's lights eye Am at last,
she dusts death from her limbs and moves toward his longing
with all deliberate speed, calling to the wind to awake and
blow cinnamon, saffron, and ginger into her garden, for she
spies his slight form almost transfigured by moonlight.

IV

At Cora's, Selah yields her room to the thorns sprouting
from the walls and the mist rising from the floor, and mixes
rum and coke with hemlock. Just as she is about to drink
and die, she stumbles upon Reverend Langford — an
exposed riverbed — sprawled in the middle of the kitchen
floor. "Why are you layin' in the floor?" she demands. He

smiles from his trance, "Can't you see I'm a nervous man?"
And death flees.

v

After Howlin' Will Shakespeare, Blind Jack Milton, and
Missouri Tom Eliot, I'm just one more dreamer to hoist a
guitar and strum Sixhiboux Delta Blues. Oh yes.

> *Don't the moon look fine, babe,*
> *Shinin' through the trees?*

Yet, saddened by fallen petals, the Sixhiboux River keens
through the hills. I fear to move lest I sink — like a
deliberate suicide — into disaster. The guitar string of river
flickers white, quivers, stretches. *Selah, hear my song of songs!*

> *Don't the moon look golden,*
> *Dazzlin' through the trees.*
> *Don't my gal look golden*
> *When she's lovin' me?*

PRELUDE

Shelley's a garden
enclosed.
She don't trust words:
men lie
to lie on top of you.

X, I know languages —
Music or Silence,
Touch or Absence —
that need no words.

My gate's open.
My fruits are pleasant.
Come and taste.

MONOLOGUE FOR SELAH
BRINGING SPRING
TO WHYLAH FALLS

I cry, in the vernacular, this plain manifesto,
No matter how many fishmen offer you their laps,
Or how contrary you are in the morning,
Or how your hair gleams like dark lightning,
Or how many lies the encyclopedia preserves,
Because, Selah, I won't play them parlour-seducer games —
Card tricks of chat, sleight-of-hand caresses —
Or stick my head in books. I love your raspy,
Backwoods accent, your laughter like ice breaking up!
I'd burn dictionaries to love you even once!
    Selah, I tell myself I come to Whylah Falls
To spy the river crocheted with apple blossoms,
To touch you whose hair fans in mystery,
Whose smile is Cheshire and shadow and bliss,
Whose scent is brown bread, molasses, and milk,
Whose love is Coca-Cola and rose petals
In a ship's cabin soaked in saltwater.
But my lies lie. My colleged speech ripens before you,
Becomes Negro-natural, those green, soiled words
Whose roots mingle with turnip, carrot, and squash,
Keeping philology fresh and tasty.

You slouch and sigh that sassy, love speech,
And aroused, very aroused, I exalt
Your decisive eyes, your definitive lips,
Your thighs that'd be emboldened by childbirth,
For when you move, every line of poetry quakes,
And I inhale your perfume — ground roses,
Distilled petals, praise your blue skirt bright
Against your bare, black legs! *You won't wear stockings!*

    I'm scripting this lyric because I'm too shy
To blurt my passion for you, Selah!
My history is white wine from a charred log,
A white horse galloping in a meadow,
A dozen chicks quitting an egg carton tomb,
But also selfish, suicidal love.
I don't want that!

    Selah, I want to lie beside you
And hear you whisper this poem and giggle.
Selah, I thought this poem was finished!
Selah, I am bust right upside the head with love!

TO SELAH

The butter moon is white
Sorta like your eyes;
The butter moon is bright, sugah,
Kinda like your eyes.
And it melts like I melt for you
While it coasts 'cross the sky.

The black highway uncoils
Like your body do sometimes.
The long highway unwinds, mama,
Like your lovin' do sometimes.
I'm gonna swerve your curves
And ride your centre line.

Stars are drippin' like tears,
The highway moves like a hymn;
Stars are drippin' like tears, beau'ful,
The highway sways like a hymn.
And I reach for your love,
Like a burglar for a gem.

LOVE LETTER
TO AN AFRICAN WOMAN

Beloved:

In my miserable weakness, I disparage you; in my childish fear, I ignore you; in my profound self-hatred, I lash out at you; in my gross ignorance, I use you, abuse you, but then can't understand why I lose you. I am stupidly contradictory — rude, when I should be respectful; cold, when I should be caring.

I want you to obey me. Why won't you? I want you to be who I think you should be. Why are you so stubborn? To ask such questions is to confess that I have lost our history.

Are you not Sheba, "black but comely," who enlightened Solomon; Nefertiti, who brought glory to Egypt; Harriet Tubman, who brandished a pistol and pledged to shoot any slave who tried to abandon her freedom train; Lydia Jackson, who fled Nova Scotian chains to found Sierra Leone; Portia White, who enthralled the world with song; Carrie Best, who gave us a *Clarion* voice; Pearleen Oliver, who brought our history on home; Marie Hamilton, whose steadfast compassion uplifted many? Are you not these heroines and a hundred more?

African daughter, forgive me my several trespasses. I have been so weak, so scared!

Black Queen, teach me to cherish children; teach me the pride of our Blackness, our Negritude; teach me that manhood is not the dumb idolatry of muscles but the impassioned sharing of love in battling injustice.

Let us make a pact: I will cease my fear; you will cease your despair.

Black Madonna! I love your African essence, your faith in children, your insatiable desire for freedom, your swift intelligence, your sharp passion, your secret strengths, your language that tells no lies, your fashion that is colour, your music that is gospel-lullaby, your lips like crimson berries, your skin like soft, moist night, your eyes like dusk, your hair like dark cotton, your scent like rich butter, your taste like raisins and dates and sweet wine.

Let us join. My love, let us join.

NIGHT TRAIN

The lean, livid engine plunges through night.
I almost feel moist softness — rain's sheer silk:
A crow wallows in this wet, cool pleasure
Like a man in his tomb, stricken numb, dumb,
By soil, its cool clench, sexual pressure.
I hug cigarette smoke, anticipate
Selah, her dark face upturned full of stars,
Her love's squeezed cotton and muscle. The town
Pulls tight. The train shudders. A sweet spasm.

BLUES FOR X

Pretty boy, towel your tears,
And robe yourself in black.
Pretty boy, dry your tears,
You know I'm comin' back.
I'm your lavish lover
And I'm slavish in the sack.

Call me Sweet Potato,
Sweet Pea, or Sweety Pie,
There's sugar on my lips
And honey in my thighs.
Jos'phine Baker bakes beans,
But I stew pigtails in rye.

My bones are guitar strings
And blues the chords you strum.
My bones are slender flutes
And blues the bars you hum.
You wanna stay my man,
Serve me whisky when I come.

ACCUMULATED WONDER

A rural Venus, Selah rises from the
gold foliage of the Sixhiboux River, sweeps
petals of water from her skin. At once,
clouds begin to sob for such beauty.
Clothing drops like leaves.

"No one makes poetry, my Mme.
Butterfly, my Carmen, in Whylah,"
I whisper. She smiles: "We'll shape it with
our souls."

Desire illuminates the dark manuscript
of our skin with beetles and butterflies.
After the lightning and rain has ceased,
after the lightning and rain of lovemaking
has ceased, Selah will dive again into the
sunflower-open river.

65

IN ACADIAN JARVIS COUNTY

I remember how Selah opened
like a complex flower.
I brushed her sleeping breasts
and they startled awake:
two, rippling fish.

She said my kisses on her breasts
were "bee stings and cool mist."
After words, I carried her, seared
with grass and kisses, from the river.

IN THE FIELD

Selah glares at me
impatiently, not seeing
the apple blossoms.

100 PROOF

Waking with a woman's name
sour and martini dry on my tongue,
I twist, lemon slice
dipped in sorrow, one-quarter asleep,
and slant, slip, slapped
to and fro like a black
bastard by alcohol's white,
wide hand; then, pasty-faced
sun whips my black back;
heat trickles bloody down my spine.
My yellow-mouthed honey creeps
'cross the linoleum in her lovin' stockin' feet.
My mouth bleeds a Bloody Mary,
song cutting my lips with liquor:
Miss Rum be my sweetest white gal,
Make me stumble from Jarvis to Whylah Falls.

ECCLESIASTES

I am tired of gold sunflowers with jade leaves.
The Sixhiboux River, almost fainting,
Weeps through the dull, deaf hills. Behind all words
Burns a desert of loneliness. Sunlight
Dulls to vulgar gold. Once I had believed
Selah's passion would seed sunflowers and yield
Skull honey — ineluctable bees' dreams.
But, all is gilt sorrow and gleaming pain:
The heavy sunflowers droop, brightness brushes
The earth; wisdom is late and death is soon.

HOW LONG CAN LOVE
GO WRONG?

You call me "serif,
lacy curlicues,
a baroque belladonna
critical men hallow."

You could never dream
my womb is gone,
hollowed by scalpels
and Casanova cancer.

I flood myself with rum,
blue smoke, and blues
to try to forget
how I've been cut.

So, tell me,
fool,
how can any poem
picture my beauty?

JORDANTOWN BLUES

At Jordantown, Selah practises love —
Hot apple pie, country and western woe,
Lash of the man away all night,
Whip of the man at work all day,
Fists of the man drunk to dumbness,
His yellow eyes flailing at nothing,
While life sags to extremes, bloodstreams, pinched, squeezed,
By his diet of white Tory rum, pig tails,
And her diet of fear, tea, and aspirin.
    Tonight, this gospel, this sermon, of a man,
Delivered by liquor, jitters, jumbles,
To their small home, chokes on a prayer of blood —
His repentance of a three-day wine binge —
And topples, comatose, to buckled knees.
He is sped, gagging, to a hospital
Where he ends, where he dies, where he stops breathing,
For Jesus comes for him through the rooftop,
Leaving Selah to practise love alone.

IV

The Passion of
Pablo and Amarantha

What is it men in women do require?
The lineaments of Gratified Desire.
What is it women in men do require?
The lineaments of Gratified Desire.

—BLAKE

THE ARGUMENT

Pablo Gabriel, thirtyish, a flamenco poet and art pedlar,
sports a slanted beret and wears rainbow cottons. His guitar
is a crescent moon. His muscular skin is orange. Amarantha
Clemence, twenty, a contemporary quilter, wears apple
blossoms in her silky, sable hair that spills — pagan-like —
down her back to her thighs. Her skin is indigo accented by
white silk.

The music of Pablo and Am segues from the Moorish
mood of Duke Ellington's "Dusk on the Desert," with its
Arabic saxophone, sobbing through oases for want of love, to
the soul cry of Bessie Smith, wailing in the Churrigueresque
temples of ecstasy. These lovers depict the struggle between
desire and despair.

A magnet hounding iron, Pablo pursues Am. Their
courtship is tense and ugly with desire. To him, her beauty
is, though clothed, always evident. Her long skirts are slit to
the thigh; her blouses are filmy. She walks in the Hollywood,
feminine way, a slight lilt in her posture, her right arm,
swinging stiffly, slightly extended from her waist. She notices
Pablo noticing her because she is ready to sew their marriage
quilt. She vanishes into a room; he lingers outside. She

leaves, brushing past him. Later, she spies him from a window and turns away. He glimpses her, rushes into the house, chases her up the stairs. Stumbles, almost falls. She gropes her door and, quick, slams it, wrenching the key in the lock. Click. He leans back, silent, then crashes through the door, collapsing into a thunder shower of blossoms or pillow feathers. Amid tears and quiet breath, their clothes flow from them, eddy, form whirlpools on the floor or cascade from the bed. Their marriage is pure Beauty. Afterwards, they cling together, forming a binary star. The radio bleats Ellington's "Crescendo and Diminuendo in Blue." Am pictures their love as the marriage of topaz and lapis lazuli.

Leaving for his old home in States County, X recognizes the soul harmony of this love. However, Jack Aurelius Thomson, former member of Parliament, famed ally of Hepburn and Duplessis, and nominated Liberal candidate for the constituency of South West Nova, yearns to make Am cry. That's his idea of music — something martial, carnal, and cacophonous.

THE HEJIRAS OF PABLO

Hating Teddy Roosevelt and his gangster Rough Riders, Pablo Gabriel fell to earth in Cuba. He sought a gentler imperialism, a haven for imagination. At thirty, he spied the word Canada in a fragment of newspaper and realized that it could be *cañada*. His atlas pictured Canada as a brown beaver (*castor canadensis*) crouched atop the grey stump of America. The beaver's foreclaws formed the strange Latin land of *Nova Scotia.* He caught a steamer to Halifax and drifted, discovering Beauty in the secret heart of the Sixhiboux Delta, that is, Whylah Falls, where dreamers, to live, gut fish, saw pine, skin mink, pick apples, or stook hay. *Whylah Falls is an ebon Muse / Whose Word is Liberty.*

Now, in his journeys from Halifax to Yarmouth, Pablo explores always the artists's utopia of Crow River. There, he crams the suitcase in his trunk with suttle sweaters, silk scarves, and postcards whose Kodachrome tints are so incandescent, they seem to leak their pictured rivers. To live, he vends these riches to the folk of Whylah Falls and all the other anti-twentieth century gardens of the Annapolis Valley. Watercolour country.

From Crow River, Pablo always follows Highway 1 west,

wending inexorably to Francis, near Jarvis, and, practising a private religion, parks at Bryant's Diner to savour Bryant Havelock's fried scallops larded with tartar sauce. Before leaving Francis, Pablo also visits Brenda's Bakery, next door to the diner. Thus, Pablo complements Bryant's cuisine with a dozen of his wife's miraculous doughnuts, tasting of spring water and sunlight.

Motoring from Francis to Whylah Falls, Pablo also stops at the Jarvis Fish and Game Club (home of stuffed trout, moose, and fiddlers), the Maillet Fire Hall (showcase of Bauhaus-style fire engines), and the Jarvis County Poor House (where Enus Cromwell gashed his leg while picking strawberries and April Branch dreamt of crossing Liberal South West Nova under stars). This schedule has determined Pablo's travels in Jarvis County since the end of his liaison with an ex-Queen Annapolisa, the exotic Cherry Dove. In those days, Pablo was searching for Beauty awarded final form.

OF MILK AND HONEY

After twelve twisted miles of gravelled
Goddamn — a back road that don't turn tricky
Into pavement until that lickety
River, the Sixhiboux, pitched with moonlight,
Dammed Kejimkujik electricity,
And baptized roses, anointed oil cans —
I've travelled this way out of strictest love
To plumb her placid, still unfathomed kiss,
Her river mouth, winding and wet, to wade
Her waters until I start to shiver —
So much milk and honey on the other side.

CLASS STRUGGLE

Bbrrrnnnngggg! Chilly 7 a.m. Stunned fingers find a slippery knob and slowly crank Annapolis Valley Radio, AVR, into a blinded room. First, however, the crackling voices of weak, American poltergeists invade, whining hurt and disaster from forlorn cities along the eastern seaboard or from God-forsaken towns locked in the eternal droughts of the mid-west. Sluggish, Amarantha clambers from her covers, swings out, her feet rediscovering the hardwood floor after a night's absence. She bathes in sunlight, the warmth heating her skin until it glows with a fine sweat. Then, she dons a silk camisole of water, letting it ripple in benediction over her skin.

For breakfast, she plucks a pear from a pine Wilfruit basket, fills a bowl with Windsor wheat puffs (which she then sweetens with Lantic sugar and drowns in Farmers' milk and Avon apple sauce), browns wheat bread baked in Berwick, larding the slices with Enn-Ess butter and Purity partridgeberry jam, and guzzles a glass of Scotian Gold apple juice, fresh from Canning, and slurps cream-beiged coffee. A Ganong chocolate completes her meal. She packs Mr. Frostee root beer, a mustard and bologna sandwich, and an apple into her lunch bag.

By 8:30 a.m., she is ready. To work in the Maritime Fish Company plant. Jack Thomson brakes his smelly truck at her door precisely at 8:35 a.m. So long as she takes the Liberal Party leaflet that her hands her with a smile (always, always smiles), she can wriggle her way into the covered back of the truck, find a seat beside the other fishplant workers, knowing them all by their distinctive morning smells of shaving lotion or cheap perfume or woodsmoke caught in rag-covered hair or by their work-ruined, gargoyle faces, and ride, jostling, to tough labour for one cent per pound of gutted fish. That's all they get. Where else can they go?

SIXHIBOUX MOTORS

The oily mechanic swears grease,
Black all over him, smears words
Against his overalls, wrenches
Dirty meanings from nuts, bolts,
Screws; filth grimes his lips.
   Jack spits, says new verbs cost a fortune
But he'll order spares from the Custom
Dialect and Language Shoppe at Church
Point, *Pointe de l'Église*, home
of Frenchy's used pronouns,
Where he'd first fixed a blonde
Seduction with blue headlights
Years before he was licensed,
Her parts, like words,
Used for whatever he pleased.

AMARANTHA / MARANATHA

Orange jack-o-lantern moon glowers. I divagate this night-flooded road, wishing on Am. Her long ebony hair glistens in writhing vines; her wrist's liquid curve tumbles darkly in clouds. The stream rushes over her voice.

She be freedom. Can I get a witness?

I'll dance the arc of corn, the leap of water, 'cos I spy Am in night's sharp plunge and pitch and roll of hay — creatures caught in the act, leaping for the privacy of bushes. Crickets crack a juicy tune and Am's hair — a nun's black habit — cascades and wild rose petals storm: blood on a wheatfield.

Why should I croon the blues of every lover since song began? To kiss Am once would be the best life possible under the sun. When morning jumps . . .

Now this barbed-wire is a vine of dark grapes; the moon, a great bowl; the pines, bedposts. And I've sprouted giant wings and a long beard. And Am's words have become plums and chrysanthemums, and her pronunciation, gold butterflies.

I'm gonna drink the moon's milky ouzo and then sip a gold glass of the sun's scotch. And when Am awakes, we'll dance in each other.

TO PABLO

In school, I hated poetry — those skinny,
Malnourished poems that professors love;
The bad grammar and dirty words that catch
In the mouth like fishhooks, tear holes in speech.
Pablo, your words are rain I run through,
Grass I sleep in.

TRANSLATED FROM
THE SPANISH

Come, my love, come, this lonely, passionate,
Nova Scotian night. Your voice trembles like wings,
Your bones whisper. Under the moon, I stroll
The shadowed road, awaiting your dark eyes
And sandalled feet. My love, if I have to,
I will pace this blue town of white shadows
And black water all night, if I have to.

I LOVE YOU/MORE THAN WORDS

Nowhere in Scripture does the unspiritual mind tread upon ground so mysterious and incomprehensible as in this text, while the saintliest men and women of the ages have found it a source of pure and exquisite delight.

—SCOFIELD

"Am, watcha doin'?" Slant eyes cut white stars in her night-smooth face. Bared, angry breasts push hard against my naked chest. Our last clothes swoon before the marvellous. I spy them broken, abandoned, somewhere. Then, water rushes us. I can see her, blurred beauty, utter *womman*, négligéed in a *chador* of water, the diaphanous veil parting around her nipples. I taste her tongue, nipples, sex, in my mouth. Body poetry and sass. *Je ne me rappelle que son pantalon à dentelles blanches.* Stop! Stop! What if someone walks in? What if . . . Water tongues us. She's smooth, slides — like rain — over me. Wind corrugates the river. My hands massaging her breasts; her hands all over my back; water making everything easy. My breath's in her hair, hers is steam against my throat where she's kissed and bitten. Water gushes over us as we finale and mmmmmmm. Sleepy John

Estes murmurs, "I Love You More Than Words Can Say."
Send our roots rain!

The language we swill with loneliness is liquor, is love, a
turmoil in the bones. Blackcurrant tea. We have forgotten
her hand-hewn beech bed, her goosedown pillow, her oceanic
quilt, her sweet deal dresser. We surge in water as if rolling
in maple leaves or as if we are entries in an encyclopedia of
flowers, a fresh garden bed. Twatching each other, we
exchange valentines of being. A gourmet trumpet dices Cajun
catfish *Bb* with Acadian trout *G#*, stewing a blues callaloo.

> *I'm gonna get some grits,*
> *gonna dip in my spoon.*
> *I'm gonna stir yer pot*
> *'til the juice run down.*

THE SONG OF LA PASIONARA

1 His mouth reaps, harvests, my kisses.
   My lips are bruised from the marks of his teeth.

2 Her hair pitches black as trees loved by winter,
   disentangled of clothing, the bare limbs, black
   and wet with the sweat of rain.

3 Clenched by a terrible sweetness, we lie
   together. Our skin is blue and orange.

4 We are water and rock: waves running back
   to the sea; rock crumbling into further sand.

5 Our eyes flood with light. We can't get enough.

THE SPRINGTIME OF
THE INNOCENTS

Sawing a logging song, Pushkin rises, meanders into wet,
tobacco blues, and gulps roses from the trumpet. Amarantha
burns incense of coffee in the crooked kitchen. I taste steam,
maybe her, or Cora's squash sprouting from the wooden
chair. I can see buds on the chair legs, and some are about
to flower.

Jack takes out his life insurance — a bottle of beer —
and pours himself a tall, cool policy. Amarantha hollers,
"Praise God, what's all the racket?" I answer, grinning, "Just
a bunch of drunken angels, Am, swimmin' through the thick
air of the senses stunned and bangin' into the floor. Some
knock on it like it's a door, but if it opens, they'll just plop
right into a dark, moist nest of worms. So, we lift 'em and
lay 'em out to dry on beds. Slowly, they resurrect, lookin'
extra beautiful and not a bit sorry."

Muscled Othello, Shakespeare of song, hums through his
harmonica, "Wherefore art thou, olde Suzanna?" until
raindrops stream from the ceiling. They look like musical
notes but they're the soft and silvery tears of innocence.
Could it be that God's cryin'? O yells out Leadbelly, "Sweet
moon, shine on, shine on!" Has Am fainted or is this just

love? She begins to fall; my arms catch her. We tumble, happy.

Maybe someone snaps fingers or the door opens. I am in a church of raspberries, sucking these proverbs. Red leaks from the roses, pours onto Am's full, Negro lips.

Later, Jack come at me out the corner of some music. Dragging the moon behind, he clambers over the woodpile and drops upon my shadow. I just laugh and scrawl more leaves for Am, maple leaves being best for love notes. Jack sways upright, slurps homely ridiculousness, bolts. Othello yaffles; the stars bawl. It's the last thing I know before I sleep.

Morning. I awake, not wanting to leave this jungle of blackberries and lilacs, wanting to sketch the candelabra of branches. So Pushkin says, "I told you; look, boy, it ain't no damn good; your feet can't lead your heart astray." Cora croons agreement: "You and Am should be sewed together like Siamese twins." Am smiles shyly, her blue skin shimmering like water, light bending through its surface tension.

Too happy, I get drunk and stagger across the Sixhiboux River, envision bullrushes as strange marijuana. I imagine that books are pools wherein meaning sinks beneath the words rippling on the surface. That's why no two readings are alike. Every breath of being that passes over a page disturbs the surface text and distorts the meaning beneath.

Back at Cora's, Missy stands up with her Jarvis County guitar, its strings pouring into the Sixhiboux, and lets her fingers ripple the blue-green river. The guitar frame hulks in sight like the Poor House; its shingles catch and rebuff her tears. A chorus is born: first, a little wail, then, a huge cry, spanked into being by Missy's own sobs.

Jack starts to get ignorant again, so Cora yells, "Not in my house!" We spill into the June night cold with white frost. Jack beats boulders, englishes blues:

> *I know you been lovin' him; yes, I can tell*
> *By your crinkled backbone, your smile that smells.*

I dream I fall on a pillow of roses, or Am, and roll in her earth like a puppydog:

> *When a man loves a woman,*
> *Can't think of nothin' else . . .*

We slow drag across the grass and then . . .

Finally, Leadbelly bays at the moon and Buck splashes in from the corner of the page, yelping for attention. Jack leaves, slamming the door. And this song is Canadian literature.

QUILT

Sunflowers are sprouting in the tropical livingroom.
Pablo, I am falling away from words.

The newspaper scares me with its gossip of Mussolini and
the dead of Ethiopia.
The radio mutters of Spain and bullets.
Only the Devil ain't tired of history.

Yesterday, I saw — puzzled beside railroad tracks — a horse's
bleached bones.
Roses garlanded the ribs and a garter snake rippled greenly
through the skull.

The white moon ripples in the darkness of fallen rain.
The sunflowers continue in the living room.
The latest reports from Germany are all bad.

I quilt, planting sunflower patches in a pleasance of thick
cotton.
I weave a blanket against this world's freezing cruelty.

LEAR OF WHYLAH FALLS

Muscular, maddened, and wrecking cornstalks,
Our Lear totters, interrogates the crows,
Keels, and rags his majesty on brambles.
Felled, green maple leaves tangle in his hair.
Imbalanced by illicit, bitter ale,
He vows he'll slog to the cold Atlantic
To sound the wrinkling and remorseless deep
That shut over the head of Lycidas,
To aquarium his queer brain in brine
Under the tumult and racket of gulls.

    Let Othello sleep now. O, lay him down,
Oceaned in silk sheets and flannel blankets,
Quilts of floribunda (a glimpse of death —
The poor sadness of pine which encloses).
Twine our fallen monarch a crown of vines
And roses (he will be beautiful in death),
And wind beside the Sixhiboux and perch
On rocks and mourn for all humanity.

UNNATURAL DISASTER

Shedding woodchips, Jack barges through the door, sidles up
to Amarantha, and presses her against him. Busy frying the
backroom in butter and vinegar so the mackerel won't feel so
naked, and enraged by his trespass, she pushes him away.
Jack shambles back in a secret frenzy of frustration that every
seam of his shirt can feel, the tension turning cotton into
iron. He breathes hard and squints right through her, ogling
lubricious mortality. He swears he'll stallion this mare.

> I come and bam on your door,
> Crack a keg of homemade nails.
> You shake your drawers in my face
> Until each bone in me howls.

Before Am can fire her fierce fists, Othello intervenes, his
voice looming out of a livingroom that Jack had forgotten
existed. Flushed, giggling, Jack flounces into the room, faces
the end-time pharaoh who sits regally in an armchair, one
hand gripping an RC Cola like a sceptre.

"You two-faced, piss-ass rat! Get out! If you say a single
black word, I'll bash your false face. I'll mash your dough

face. Sweep up your woodchips, scarecrow, and disappear."
Othello's words settle soft as love notes.

Am lets the fish sizzle in the dry air, passes Jack the broken broom, and, noticing his nasty frown, warns, "No use clouding up; you can't rain." Jack sweeps, hallucinates a death.

> He wash his face in a fryin' pan;
> He comb his head with busted glass.

TWO DREAMS

I trapped a Queen of Spain butterfly, its wings marbled with veins of gold and red, and placed it in my pocket inside a match-box. Then, Pablo and I tramped through the dusky woods to the river.

We watched the water fall all that evening. All that evening, we were pestered by butterflies — Orange Tigers and White Admirals — that fluttered about and settled upon us.

I drifted into a dream. Othello had been shot. I saw his blood glaring in the grass.

A knife fell into my left hand. Scratch Seville stood before me and ripped off his white shirt. I sliced him so bad that when they picked him up to place him on the stretcher, he came apart in their hands.

Then, I was standing, haloed by butterflies, on a scaffold. Someone tugged a rope around my neck, and I jerked into space.

I awoke, screaming, and Pablo gathered me to his warmth. I awoke, screaming, and Pablo gathered me to his warmth.

V

The Martyrdom of
Othello Clemence

Three gushes of blood,
and he died in profile.
Living coin which never
will be repeated.

—GARCIA LORCA

THE ARGUMENT

Othello Clemence's martyrdom is cold realism. Thus, when he is shot, the mortal moment must be filmed from above and below, from behind and in front, from left and from right, in slow motion, normal speed, and fast, in close-up, and from a telescopic distance. The completeness of history must be depicted. Clemence must be photographed amid a chaos of primary colours which, at the split second he is shot, bleed to black-and-white. At that precise moment too, his guitar must be splintered upon a rock, freeing the twenty-four pale butterflies trapped behind the strings.

While the news of Clemence's death echoes from the reports of the shotgun, three Mounties, wearing scarlet tunics, saddle three sable horses. The camera cuts from them to a grainy shot of Clemence's mother, Cora, wailing in her kitchen while Blind Lemon Jefferson's "Bad Luck Blues" twists lazily on an out-of-focus phonograph.

S. Scratch Seville, the murderer, dresses wholly in white, including a white tie and gloves, but his gun is a serpentine black. He is about forty, with rotten teeth and a beard stuck like bread mold to his face. His eyes are dead. He stinks of homicide. When he fires point-blank into Clemence, blasting him through the door, there is no sound but his own fast heartbeat.

The sound of the blast ricochets later in unexpected places. It is heard when S. S. S. is acquitted from the murder charge. It is heard again when an orchestra of typewriters performs *Otello* for two hundred thousand tabloids in three cities. Seville is a nightmare cartoon. After his acquittal, he dissolves to flowers.

The shot — a meteor — strikes X in States County. Shelley feels its impact as she rides the Flying Bluenose upshore for a weekend visit.

A VISION OF ICARUS

Ecce ipsi idiote rapiunt celum ubi
Nos sapientes in inferno mergimur.

—ST. AUGUSTINE

Moonlit, glimmering like each mortal dream,
Othello tries the air with patchwork wings,
Plummets through vast nightmare, then smacks the chill
Channel of black, thrashes in amnesia,
Flounders, encumbered by eels and current.
Adreynten, he becomes our Icarus,
Ravelled by lilies, laved by the river,
His auburn ankles shackled by sawgrass.

    When Pablo fishes our king from the ooze,
His bones will be chalk, his skull, gypsum,
His eyes, amethyst isled in ambergris.
We'll comb periwinkles from his bleached hair,
And pick the early pearls from his bared ribs.
·Those who'd wing with angels do often drown.

FOUR GUITARS

Pushkin, Othello, and Pablo gather in the livingroom coral reef, under a sea of sunshine, to perform improv music (no note knowing where the next is going to or coming from). They lean over their guitars like accountants studying thick ledgers.

Casting half-notes, thirds, and quarter-notes that stretch music like putty, Pushkin opens the concert. He bends the long metre of Baptist hymns into infernal hollers that true Baptists are sure the wicked Anglicans and Catholics enjoy behind the dark doors of their temples. From "If All the World Were Apple Pie," a nursery rhyme, he dredges sedimentary notes laden with a sorrow as rich as that felt by Schliemann who discovered Troy because he was looking for love and the lost city got in his way.

Desperate for his own private sound, Pushkin once crafted a banjo from a frying pan and four pieces of string. Favouring *E* or *A* notes, plucking them — luscious fruit, heavy with memory and tears — from his American Martin guitar, he stands before us now, revelling in an *abb* rhyme scheme, the cadence of decadence:

April rain snows white and cold,
I feel so goddamn scared.
You could've loved me if you'd dared.
Were you waitin' to get old?
Why did you act so weird?
You loved me like you never cared!

Next, he plumbs the depths of bottomless love, "Don't do
me evil / If you want the sun to shine," holding a breadknife
against the throat of the guitar, forcing forth bastard slurs
and mongrel fluctuations, a lover's midnight moans. He
slides his stopping finger on the string, contrasting long notes
with quick arpeggios, then backs into "Black Liquor" with
fierce fluidity. Forgetting that his hands are warped, he plays,
plagued by the currency of the radio cantos of Ezra
"Epopee" Pound: *I love my baby, love her to the bone.* Like
Don Messer and his Famous Islanders, Pushkin cannibalizes
cacophony. When he attains zen-silence, hullabaloo collapses
the room. He empties a bottle — a backward song — down
his throat, smiles like sudden, brilliant snow.

Lean Othello follows the sweating giant, steps into the
wake of his lilt and the still fluttering applause. He snatches
his Dobro-chrome, steel-bodied guitar, tunes it Sebastopol
style, dreaming that that's where William Hall won the
Victoria Cross more than a hundred years ago. O chooses
"Hurry Down, Sunshine," then discards it because the room

is bright enough. He selects, to a chorus of whoops and thigh slaps, "Black Water Blues." He lays the guitar gently across his hips, presses the supine strings with a tall, brown bottle, and plays, thus sending quirky notes, tottering like drunken flowers, into the air. In the corner, Pushkin gasps, "Ooh!" O's artistry is that fine. His elegant left-hand figures, instrumental algebra, merge with his rough, dark voice:

> I bought ya red, red, calico:
> mmmmmmm, ya didn't love me though.

> Moon burnt the blue sky orange;
> not ripe, plucked stars tasted green.
> In its hard bed, the river tossed, black.

> God made everyone with a need to love;
> wonder who ya be thinkin' of?

His waterfall-hands cascade across the strings, leave, behind the glistening notes, a dark, inarticulate silence.

Unable to restrain himself, Pablo tunes his flamenco guitar Spanish style, nudging O into a Latinate version of "I bes troubled." Pablo contributes his exotic expertise, his Moorish sense to that spiritual salvaged from two centuries of bad luck. His music tastes of three little feelings: saltiness, bitterness, and sweetness. Reminiscing in tempo, Othello pursues Pablo's anxious influence. Stressing static sadness by inverting the scale of flattened third and seventh degrees, they distort prettily Robert Johnson's classic blues, "Hell Hound."

Suddenly, Pablo discovers music drowned in a seashell and raises it, sounding as polished and suave as the clear, hairless limbs of the Chinese, Spanish, and Jamaican women he loves, women with indigant breasts, shell-smooth skin, and opulent thighs. While he plays, the Sixhiboux River shimmies silver through the hills, lindys beneath the bridge, and jitters into Saint Mary's Bay. He uncaps a bottle of Keith's India Pale Ale, *brewed the same way for a hundred years*, and nods in the direction of *Nisan*:

> *Thirty days of daffodils,*
> *Lilies, and chrysanthemums,*
> *Open with snowy petals*
> *And close with apple blossoms.*

O follows, remembering the lost music of sub-Saharan Africa and trying to perfect the blues.

When this chance duet fades, leaving clear notes hanging, untended, in the air, Missy barges in, panting, yammers, "Quit the gentle mercies and the delicate fears! God expects truth, not entertainment!" She unfolds a dark mandolin, rich, smelling of drenched forests, then jumbles the room into shape around her, juggling it so it becomes circular, curling around her curves. "Who's got a cigar box and string? A diddley bow?" Silence. Then, Pushkin, his breath renewed, manifests a ten-hole, twenty-reed, Marine Band harmonica, commences to mock a train, a historic freight, stuffed with Southern sunflowers, Mississippi magnolias. Missy adopts Poor Girl tuning, mumbles her debt to Bessie Smith and Amy "Big Mama" Lowell, booms, "I've got Ford engine movements in my hips."

I look outside. The sun has turned inside out. Moonlight lacquers the world. Black bliss. Missy trolls an immortal song:

> Come and love me, darling one,
> In sweetest April rain.
> Kiss me until life is done:
> Youth will not come again.

ON JUNE 6TH

Othello stood with friends
amid lush, fiery leaves,
tested intricate white
lightning, writhing like lithe
vipers in cages of glass.
Had he dreamt his soon death,
he would have contemplated
carbon culture:
how skin and bones
become diamonds
after so much pain.
It is our fate
to become beautiful
only after tremendous pain.

SEVILLE

PERSONS OF THE DIALOGUE
Scratch Seville & Jack Aurelius Thomson

SCENE

Seville and Thomson conclave at a crippled table in Seville's shack. Seville, garbed in milk-white, downs a beer, smokes cigs, wipes sweat from his brow. Thomson, wearing a dun suit and fisher boots, sips Scotch from a tumbler he keeps eyeing for dirt. Kerosene lamp light corrodes the kitchen.

Seville: After ya told me how that black pup, Othello, threatened ya over Ama, I went and told Cora, "If ya don't want someone lookin' at yer friggin', long-chin daughter, keep her at home." Jack, them Clemences ain't nothin' but coloured trouble. I told Cora straight, "Ya ain't got no sense, ya must be missin' half a head." Then the yella-mouthed half-and-half sasses me, sayin', "Get out ma house! Ya usetabe okay but now ya've turned the opposite — aggravatin', mean-minded, cross-eyed and grouchy!" Then she called Angel a whore and said our boy ain't mine.

Thomson: You honoured your honour?

Seville: Well, I was jes 'bout to smack her silly when that big oaf of hers, Othello, lumbers in and suckers me. That bastard hit me so hard, I figured I'd been cracked with a two-by-four. And then he drawls, "If I ever spy ya shadowin' our doorway again, mister man, I'll put a beatin' on ya that you'll never take off!"

Thomson: You let that scalawag shame you?

Seville: Well, I've never been good-fisted. If I'd had my gun then, it woulda been holy slaughter, 'cos I coulda blowed off his head and grinned while doin' it; and if Cora'd fussed, she woulda had a close call to the Devil's arms!

Thomson: Ha! Ha! Ha!

Seville: What's the big joke?

Thomson: That tomcat's sniffing around your little pussy, Angel. I heard him tell Eely that "There must be something in the milk for girls to have asses like that."

Seville: I'll blast his head off if he jes' blinked at her!

BEFORE THE SHOT

A "lie," Othello?
A fact: Jack Thomson saw you,
last night, man my wife.

DEATH SONG

The shotgun splutters loneliness,
Its loneliness, black like the sea.
A guitar breaks, and twenty-four
Yellow butterflies flutter free.
We are but dust.

I hear the leaden, dismal moan
Of metal mourning for the flesh:
Milk that creams upon blancmange bones,
Honey that cakes in sugar skulls.
We are but dust.

The Atlantic mutters, then mewls,
Tearing itself from rough gravel.
My blood waters grass and gravel,
My tears baptize stones with the sea.
We are but dust.

THE LONESOME DEATH OF
OTHELLO CLEMENCE

A bootlegger blasts. Othello's life shines.
It sputters free in red, blubbering air.
His giant hands palm crimson misery,
Try to patch his stomach. Fingers bandage
The lead-bored hole but nothing can stop Death.
The wind swoops low to kiss and sponge his brow
And haul a fiery quilt of stars over
His weary head; crows shred their wings in thorns;
He sips vinegar-tears. His history,
Giddying through a gyre, a puckered hole
In his stomach, stops on bloodied gravel
While silence whines in the legislature.

REVOLUTIONARY EPOCH

The motor of music breaks down in dirt
And gravel for Othello wheels and falls
Face down in sorrow and his last white wine,
Regret pale like lightning or arthritis
In his bones. He is clear rigor mortis,
Falling like a redwood or a river
Staggering down a shocked mountainside.
His drunken nerves panic and faint. He dreams
He'll ebb to gold beneath lilies and grass.
      Pablo sinks into his river guitar,
Scrounges for Beauty until melody
Evaporates, casting up string as still
And white a bone. He remembers his fist
In O's mouth, the motor dead in his car.
Cora folds in her armchair, still holding
Her final rum — that pale, pocket Bible.
Skeletal, arthritic lightning staggers;
Electricity panics, faints, and fails.
Through the traumatized landscape, a train lopes
Like a *loup-garou*, baying at the moon.

THE WAKE

Cora stammers her pain in a white poem
Of rum more eloquent than speech; her fists
Daze, totter, the crippled maple table,
Shatter glasses in sudden homicide.
She lowers her noble head and ululates
Until her clear face glistens like the sea.
Her first-born son is lost. Now, there's nothing.
There's nothing left but life insurance.

    Cora lumbers to the twisted window,
Watches wet, yellow sunlight flood the grass
And raise buttercups, daisies, marigolds.
She yearns to soak O's limbs in gold perfumes
Of myrrh and frankincense to erase death —
The dark, earth odour of potato peels
And damp, moldy leaves. She wants him to rise,
Gilt and garlanded. She wants him to rise.

EULOGY

His breath went emergency in his lungs,
His felled heart grasped impossibly at light;
A thrown bouquet, he dropped softly to earth.
Torn from sweet oxygen, O wilted fast.
    We have now come to bury our beloved.
We stumble through smoke, broken sentences,
Snatch fresh, pale lilies from his dark bier,
Watch water smash its white brains on black rocks.
    Children, all deaths concentrate in this one.
The rain now falling is each, single tear.

SEVILLE GRANTED BAIL

By Biter Honey

HALIFAX — Bail has been granted to S. Scratch Seville, pending his trial on a charge of second degree murder in the June shotgun slaying of a 30-year-old man at Maillet, Jarvis County.

Mr. Justice Pious Cutthroat of the Nova Scotia Supreme Court rejected a Crown request to keep Seville, 40, in custody until he faces trial this autumn for allegedly killing Othello Clemence.

The Crown lawyer Fiskal Wyse opposed bail in a Halifax hearing, citing the "apparent scandal" that would pertain if an accused murderer were freed without regard for public perception.

Mr. Justice Cutthroat granted Seville's release on $100 bail, without cash or property as security, noting the background of the case indicated the victim had been an "evil drunk."

Seville will be tried in Jarvis in October.

MAN DROWNS IN SIXHIBOUX RIVER

A 25-year-old Beulah Pines man drowned early yesterday morning after his pine raft overturned in rapids on the Sixhiboux River near Whylah.

Ovide Vendredi slid beneath twelve feet of violent water at about 12:12 a.m.

Whylah Constable Eymeric Coffin said a cottager – noted poet, William Henry Drummond – heard cries for help and found the raft, a black beret, and a paddle.

"It is fairly disruptive water there," Drummond said, "where the Sixhiboux pours down its fierce, resistless flood."

*

OUR MISTAKE

Ex-MP Jack Thomson was mis-identified in a photo appearing in last week's *Moon*. The photo was of the new Jarvis Sewage Treatment Plant. The *Moon* regrets the error.

*

Last week's recipe for Whylah Falls Apple Pie should have listed the ingredients as including seven peeled apples *not* potatoes. The *Moon* regrets the typographical error.

Scratch Seville is free pending murder trial. MOON PHOTO

THE TESTIMONY OF
OTHELLO CLEMENCE

When I felt the scream as the shot smoked . . . and saw the
hot, red pain as it tore my stomach, splashing me back
through the soft door that crumpled like thin ice, icy
splinters gouging my back, and I flailed under air, I swore
Seville had drowned me. I was at peace. But that peace was
pissed by terror as I crawled down his thrashing driveway,
wanting water. Water. I was leaking from a savage hole in my
stomach, my face busted, and the sight in my eyes crazy,
blue, red, yellow, I wasn't much able to move, then I blurred
Scratch limping slow after me, cursing his fucked door, and
looming over me (I ain't lyin') with his butterknife (I know,
pretty funny, 'cept it wasn't very funny for me), and drove
the cold blade into my gut so hard he bent the tip.

All I could think about was having surgery. I imagined
the lead was removed, bone and metal fragments sifted from
good tissue and organs, part of my left thigh bone, pulverized
by the weird discharge, removed and replaced with wood, my
severed spleen sewn, the holes in my stomach and bowel
repaired, a tube inserted in my chest to reinflate my lung
which had collapsed when the chest cavity was pierced by the
butterknife's upward twist. I could almost smell the clean

linen, the perfumed, white nurses; could almost hear my buddies joshing me, "Lazarus."

But it was just a dream. What happened was horror. Helped by Jack (that sleeveen who was screwing Seville's old lady, Angel), Seville didn't once stop his attack on me. Quite the contrary. The simple bastard broke my stomach at very close range. That was the only evil in the shotgun, and he knew it. When he feared it had failed, he must have gone to his kitchen, gone straight to the knife drawer, and got a butterknife, knowing it would follow the lead into my gut and leave no trace. Does that sound as though he killed in self-defence?

Make no mistake! Seville used that knife to stab me. And when I whimpered, he stabbed me again. And when blood, instead of words, spilled from my mouth, he stabbed me again and again, and he would have gone on stabbing me 'til I was dead, 'cept he was scared someone would come. But it didn't matter 'cause I died anyway.

THIS WORLD IS PASSING AWAY

Night wields its death blow, nullifying
The trains that writhe across this map, stilling
The crows that crack the air with blackened cries.
Cora mourns her son, Othello Clemence,
Who, shot down by Scratch Seville, dreamt and bled
Too much. He dropped in the garden where he
Had crawled, bowled over, like a dog. Then, bright,
Enthusiastic machines stormed his last
Self defence with morphine. In court, Scratch joked,
"Self-defence." His white-wash jury guffawed.

   No death is neutral anymore.

THE BALLAD OF OTHELLO CLEMENCE

There's a black wind howlin' by Whylah Falls;
There's a mad rain hammerin' the flowers;
There's a shotgunned man moulderin' in petals;
There's a killer chucklin' to himself;
There's a mother keenin' her posied son;
There's a joker amblin' over his bones.
Go down to the Sixhiboux River, hear it cry,
"Othello Clemence is dead and his murderer's free!"

O sang from Whylah Falls and lived by sweat,
Walked that dark road between desire and regret.
He pitched lumber, crushed rock, calloused his hands:
He wasn't a saint but he was a man.
Scratch Seville shot him and emptied his skull,
Tore a hole in his gut only Death could fill.
Now his martyr-mother witnesses in cries
Over his corpse cankered white by lilies.

There's a black wind snakin' by Whylah Falls;
There's a river of blood in Jarvis County;
There's a government that don't know how to weep;

There's a mother who can't get no sleep.
Go down to the Sixhiboux, hear it moan
Like a childless mother far, far from home,
"There's a change that's gonna have to come,
I said, a change that's gonna have to come."

THE HISTORY OF DEATH

When I heard, I mean, when I understood what happened
to Othello, the air caught fire and the sun burnt black.
I couldn't breathe. Pushkin took raw music from his pockets,
mixed it with Red Man tobacco, tamped both into his pipe,
lit it, and blew red smoke into the fierce air. I gulped hot,
tear-laden oxygen.

Time failed. Numbers peeled from clocks. I forgot the
promise of rain to wipe away every tear. I felt that if I moved
a single bone, I would shatter.

Reverend Langford came by, I remember, told me, after
the fire had died from the air, to stare at the stars. I did.
I did. Then, he charted the history of death and said that if
I wanted peace, all I need do was connect the right stars —
like dots — and God's serene, holy face would appear. And
I did and I fell sleepy and a great peace came down.

— Shelley

WHEN WILL DEATH DIE?

They kept Othello unburied over Sunday until Monday. Now, why'd someone do something so stupid? Whenever that happens, someone else is doomed to die. That's practical gospel, sister.

Well, at the funeral at Whylah Falls African Baptist Church, there was all this hootin' and weepin' and wailin' and flailin' of fans. Folks was standin' and singin' and tears was droppin'. You should've seen it. Oh, look, girl, it was too much for Ol' Cassiopeia Israfel who steamered all the way back from the Boston States for the ceremony.

Well, she jumps up on her fourscore-year-old legs, shakin' the big ol' gangly flowers on her black felt hat, steps out from the pew, folks grabbin' at her to get her to sit, warnin', "Yer too old! You'll hurt yourself!" and she says, "Lemme be! I babysat that boy!" And so she starts bawlin' and yellin' 'bout how terrible ugly life is, and how death is just 'cos it brings the peace of God and you get to go home and lay your head on Christ's soft bosom, and even Rev. Langford was clappin' and amenin' with her 'cos she clear had the Spirit, and the whole church was so quiet, you could hear the tears streamin'. Then, her voice just run out, and she stood up as straight as she could get herself, and stretched out her arms to God as if she could see Him floatin' over the choir, and then she just fell, and was dead — just like that.

Lord, have mercy. When will death die?

— Lavinia Jarvis

THE LONESOME DEATH OF OTHELLO CLEMENCE

Snapping like clay, his bones refuse to hold;

His body's doors burst wide; blood floods from fresh

Exits, leaving only tears — a white mob

Of rain pummeling a lynched, black branch.

Soon, Pushkin will furrow black, yielding earth

And bury the white moon, and Reverend

Langford demand, "Has God fled to some star?"

And Scratch plod miles to Beulah Pines, his shoes

Spiflicated, the sides all busted out,

And newsmen — typewriters banging, banging,

Shotgun Othello again and again,

Until scarecrows' straw heads splinter against

Lead skies or ruin in rain, and news yellows

To history and he is duly dead.

VISION OF JUSTICE

I see the moon hunted down, spooked from hills,
Roses hammer his coffin shut, O stilled
By stuttered slander, judicial gossip,
And a killer's brawling bullet. Bludgeoned
Men, noosed by loose law, swing from pines; judges,
Chalked commandants, gabble dour commandments;
Their law books yawn like lime-white, open pits
Lettered with bones, charred gibberish, of those
Who dared to love or sing and fell to mobs.
Language has become volatile liquor,
Firewater, that lovers pour for prophets
Whom haul, from air, tongues of pentecostal fire —
Poetry come among us.

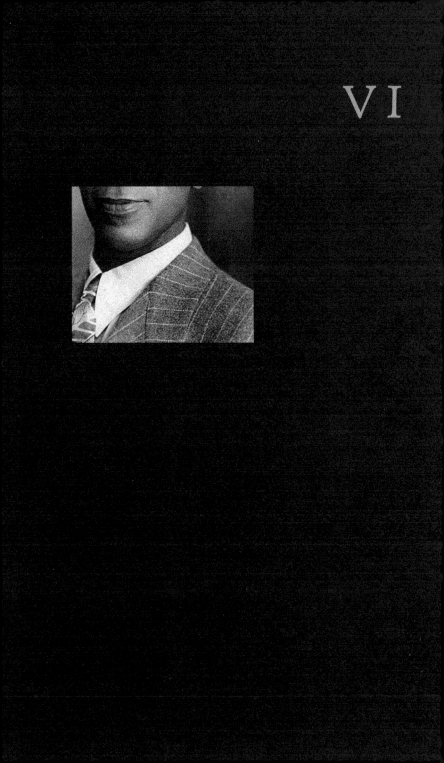

VI

The Gospel of
Reverend F. R. Langford

This is the book of man "under the sun,"
reasoning about life; it is the best man can do,
with the knowledge that there is a holy God,
and that He will bring everything into judgment.

—SCOFIELD

THE ARGUMENT

Poor immigrant! If only, if only, if only, this land were not
rosedust where the first fathers sleep, he would be mayor or
county warden or even premier now. Instead, he spreads
crisp newspapers like maps and plots politics, discovering
archipelagos of *bons mots* amid the black-and-white seascape of
scandals and crises. He stares at the grey photograph of
Othello Clemence in the obituary section and remembers his
own one-third African, one-third Mi'kmaq, and one-third
English inheritance, the reasons for his copper skin, straight-
black hair, cinnamon eyes, and wide mouth. Reverend
Franklin Roosevelt Langford, born without a memory of the
Rt. Hon. Sir John A. Macdonald, the bastard hanging of
Louis Riel, or the Boer War election of 1900, believes
everyone is an alien, a refugee, *un émigré*. Everyone emigrates
to the world from his or her mother. Heaven is everyone's
true home. The gospel according to Rev. Capt. William
Andrew White.

He turns from the newspapers, divines the perfume from a
distant, fragile flower. He hears Portia White trill, from the
phonograph, "Ride on, King Jesus," and remembers God
moulded the world from clay, wind, lightning, and rivers.

He has the serene composure, the relaxed but perfect
posture, of a man who has lived his whole life as a symbol
— *God's High Commissioner to the World*. No wonder he
scents himself with rosewater and beebalm, studies
martyrdom, fasts steadily on wine, and shouts proverbs from
house to house: "The rivers of corruption course through the
fields of innocence!" Langford prays thrice a day, facing east
towards France, Sierra Leone, China.

He considers Whylah Falls to be New Eden, the lost
colony of the Cotton Belt. He indulges in Latin because it is
as mysterious as God. Truly, he spent his youth copying the
ways of God, becoming omnipotent, omniscient, and
omnipresent whenever he chose. Sometimes, for fun, he
would appear out of nowhere, wrapped in blinding flame,
and frighten lovers meeting in compromising assignations in
dark, secret forests. Eventually, he learned to appreciate
passion, gazing upon watercolours of St. Theresa of the
Roses and St. Joan of Arc every night before he slept. He
would dream that they were his holy lovers although he was a
perfect Baptist, brought under the saving waters of the
Sixhiboux River when he was seven years old, fully immersed
as the Bible teaches, amid murmurings of Latin and long-
forgotten spirituals that sounded like the moaning of many
doves. Liana Jarvis had been there, a young woman in
dazzling white. *Were you there when they crucified my Lord?*

For Langford,
love is death's counterpoint.
Shelley and X will have to discover
for themselves this key to salvation.

THE BOY DREAMS HIS DESTINY

This bright night,
freed trains holler happiness,
Harriet Tubman history,
dust to diamonds destiny,
while the world whelms my dreams,
summons me to part books,
force time to know my name.

THIS GIVEN DAY

Morning yawns, the sun stretches, and the train
Pitches the air with smoke, paws the iron earth,
Tracks its big city game along the coast,
Narrows the span between our birth and death.
From dreams, we, *dépaysés*, fall to coffee,
Orange Free State oranges, new news, fresher dreams,
Prophesying what tomes we now must read,
What names we will need, what gods we will prize.
    All we can prove is the sun and the bay
And the baying hunter that is the train,
All joined in a beautiful loneliness —
Separated from our pure world of wounds,
Our globe of love (sharp nails hammered through palms),
Happening alone, as if it matters.

A SERMON TO THE UNDECIDED

Sinners, hear the loud sun cryin' awake with freight train howl 'cos it'll be a bit like that when great Christ come cleavin' the cloudy air to thunder love all over His precious Creation. I wanna tell you, 'cos God don't lie, that Christ is gonna catch the scarlet and purple women and the prophesyin' drunkards by surprise. Yep! When they be playin' poker, gigglin' and tee-heein' all night, they won't notice the Sun glarin' at 'em 'til it's too late and they is proved palpable fools.

How you'll be, boy, when you spy the King of Glory, brighter than the high-noon river, through rum-yellowed eyes? Will you just stumble, mumble, pass out? King Jesus says, "Woe unto you!" And how'll you be, girl? Will you be shoutin' "Hallelujah!" with scandal kisses stainin' your wine-purpled lips? Woe unto you!

Children of God, doncha know that your every breath drags through dirt? Doncha know that death overshadows you? All you want are barbecues and holidays. You don't want the House of God. You complain about this mouldy bread and the watered-down wine. You say that this commandment is too hard, this commitment too much. I say: Dirty your knees in the worship of the Lord!

Little children, get right with King Jesus! Olive Christ ain't lynched or nailed to stiff lumber. Christ is mighty! Sinners'll spy 'im by the Sixhiboux tramplin' down the lumber kings. They'll spy 'im descendin' over the sawmill, inspiring holy horror. What good will runnin' do? You can run to them Boston States, but you can't run from your sinful self!

Preach out your Bible! God says, "Love one another." Love satisfies. Love is the only thing that can't be oppressed. If any try to deny love, why, that's when the stones would tear free from their graves and howl disgust at our implicit trusts! You gotta feel love, live it, and make it true. It's not enough to be in the right church, you gotta be in the right pew!

Sinners, come home to King Jesus! Remember gold streets, sweet pastures, and doves by the river of waters. Come home, little children, to that land of milk and honey, where you don't need no passport or money. Come home!

> We're gonna shine in the fiery storm;
> We're gonna dance on the starry shore;
> We're gonna shout Christ's gloried name;
> Praise God! None of us will be the same!

THE SERMON OF LIANA

A silver Sixhiboux, the Gospel glints.
Langford stakes the Bible, sights lustrous ore,
Flustering gems. Mining, he finds that Christ,
A carpenter, made lumber hiss its lust
For air, riveted rain to riverbeds.
Langford lectures, "In the name of Heaven . . ."
But forgets the other names for heaven —
Daisy, lily, the River Sixhiboux,
Or even Liana and Langford.

    Once he completes, pebbles and boulders burst
Into blossom, lifelong drunkards sober,
The brilliant sun centres, brands him with light.
Yet, he's blinded by words, can't see that love
Is all that created and keeps our world.

141

MEMORIES OF THE HOLY BIBLE

1 Thrice have I walked amid its verdant, leafy thought, and wheatfield imagery, and heard God's voice in every breath of song, and seen His face reflected in every shining, human face.

2 And battered by voices crying alms in my ears, I have ascended its Mount Eulah to be shaken by God's voice distilled in an *F* note although magic died on the day after Pentecost.

3 And in the wild, green passages of the Bible, its flowered tracts, I have rambled with bark-brown, wild-bearded Elijah, and feasted on vinegar'd mackerel and wet strawberries.

4 And I have watched him climb Mount Eulah and vanish in fog, thick fog, falling off the pined coast.

5 And there, I have lain with Liana, black and comely, in sweet pastures.

6 And, until the dusk of dawn, we have watched the moon blossom, silvering the river and the ox-cart in the gravel pit.

7 And I emerge from the scriptures' Annapolis Valley meadows, streams, and mountains, always reborn, knowing that every word is a bible, bearing the lightning of genesis and the thunder of revelation.

THE LADIES AUXILIARY

Never cross the Ladies Auxiliary. Implacable, peppermint-scented old women, whose faces tuck into smiles or amens; young women, who stare critically at the minister and deacons and male choir soloists, perch — a row of jurors — upon hard, mahogany pews, sport impossible hats, brandish funeral parlour fans, and administer deft, surreptitious elbow jabs to fidgeting, Sunday School sinners. These women rule the church.

They stir their voices in storms of song so the stained-glass trembles, the church quakes, and the voice of God rollicks out of the pulpit so you can't help but pray. Ancient Egyptian priestesses, these women guard the sanctuary of mystery. No one cometh unto salvation save through them.

Their eyes laugh when they call, "Sister this, sister that," or comb their children's heads with stiff, painful combs or hotcombs. According to their Gospel, none of God's children dare sit in church with a nappy or picky head. And none dare sit with ashy legs. Gotta rub lemon juice on 'em. Make blackness shine.

Backsliders and sinners get cuffed upside the head or 'buked to shame. And who'd dare chat in church? Gotta prove respect. That's what faith is all about.

MUTABILITY

Is the world now ending or beginning?
The stars keep time; lovers still moan in beds.
Yet, many are shaken by appearance
And cannot see the sense of anything.
Death is all around us; Death's everywhere.
We are mere waving grass, momentary
Lightning, the dead already forgotten.
Thus, I cannot make love without trembling
Nor watch my woman give birth to hope
Without suicide sadness shaking me.
I hardly think I compass solid earth.
Those dreading faith, those without God, plummet
Into fathomless graves. I barely stand.

Is the world now ending or beginning?

THE SUTRA OF LIANA

I saw a black man who was half-fire.
I saw a white woman who was half-fog.
I remember Joe Howe's secret bastard:
He wore long hair that dropped past his shoulders
and he Cunarded the seven seas.
Father Preston galloped through four-sided weather
when he came to baptize Whylah Falls.
His face was lightning and his hands were bronze.
He brought us black bibles and blackberry jam.
His first wife, Leila, changed into a butterfly
because he was away in America too long.
This Spanish lady, Corinna, had gold teeth
and mice in her hair.
She cursed the Clear Grits and the Tories.
One winter, there was no summer.
One summer, the ground was matted with rotting fish.
The boughs of trees were draped with bodies
of decaying eels.

The old books open like moth wings.

I was born in Nictaux Falls.

I grew up surrounded by witnesses.

I brewed spring rain tea from the quick freshes.

I fell in love with a jug of red wine

on a table lit by candles and sunflowers.

I still cry when I think about, when I think about,

Othello's long legs and his beautiful feet.

His skin was black like rose petals.

He vowed to lave me every day in fresh milk

and cloak me every night in lucid silk.

Because his skin was black like rose petals,

the constables fancied he was evil.

After he was shot down, I found his blood-stained shirt.

Every day I bring candles and sunflowers to his grave.

Soon, I will pass to the dark side of the sea

beyond the waves.

RESPONSIVE READING

To sing Nova Scotia, its epic heroes of Glooscap,
Champlain, Preston, and Howe, there must needs howl an
angry train and the sharp-toned voices of African Baptist
choirs, those Black saints swaddled in snow-white robes of
Glory, testifying to Ethiopia's gorgeous blackness.

There must needs roar *Freedom's* passionate urgency, the
revolutionary cry of the Atlantic's surf storming a barricade
of rock, and the revelation cry of Black angels, wailing for
Justice, scorching the heavens above Paradise!

Nova Scotia, sometimes I need to tremble!

There must needs be the soiled yell of the fishman,
"Maaackerel, fresh maaackerel!" the earthy growl of the
greens man, "I got cabbage and lettuce for pennies," the
crooned lullaby of the midwife, "Hush-a-by, doncha cry,"
and the loud moan of the mother, "Who done shot my baby
down?"

There must needs be the shouts of house parties, the
whoop and cackle of folks too blue to cry. Angered by whip
and lash of joblessness, maddened by gun and jail of politics,

these souls clap hands and sing, "What did I do / To be so black and blue?"

Nova Scotia, God bless the child who got his own!

There must needs be the jazz swoon of joy, the river baptismals, the psalms of Easter and Christmas and wedding merriness and birth happiness, the immortal banjo and fiddle hymns — "Skip to my Lou," "Ain't Gonna Study War No More," and country-and-western rhythm and blues.

There must needs be, in the beginning and at the end, the barbed-wire spirituals of this stony peninsula — "Swing Low, Sweet Chariot" and "Farewell to Nova Scotia," a steelyard tune that Cape Bretoners chant in taverns from Moncton to Coquitlam.

We love you, Portia White!

These are the seeds of song, after the campaign bottles of rum, the liquored sentiments, the gospel-hurt sermons, the potato patch and hogfarm testaments, the coloured prophets and Beautiful Ones who kneel before the Atlantic to voice that endless chorus of fire, "I wish, oh Lord, I wish that *Truth* and *Liberty* might flower in this stony soil under these cold, hard stars."

TO THE GOVERNMENT OF NOVA SCOTIA

In this granite country, this home
Of hard rock and harder water,
Cattle trudge cold across hills, then slump
In snow — deep, dark, and constant like pain.
Winter prospers, fattening on bones.
I waste my strength in dreams and drink;
My days, in woodlots that are jails.
My one true love is a pension;
My messiah, a bingo prize.
I own but muscle, wine, and wind.
    Yet, in my heart's imagination,
I watch wild geese fly, fly,
To thatched colonies of refuge
Founded and fortressed in Tantramar marsh
Far from any possible hunters.
I lust for wings —
Grand impossibilities possible —
To inherit not earth, but *Heaven*.

THE SWEET SCIENCE

Politics? Bah! Another word for boxin'! There ain't no
difference between 'em. You place your bet and you put your
money down, hopin' 'gainst hope that your faith will go the
distance. Why, Joe Howe and Angus MacDonald are just
like our champs, Kid Chocolate and Buddy Daye. Lookit,
the legislature, Province House, is just a boxin' ring. Watch
the premier bob and weave, tryin' to duck the long reach and
nasty left hook of *Principle*. Reporters? They're promoters.
Lemme tell you, only suckers trust in these rigged bouts
called elections. Stevenson called it right:

> *The world is so full of a number of things,*
> *I'm sure we should all be as happy as kings.*

MORTALITY

Crows collapse into a still wind of bones,
Their black, feathered truth stripped to a white dream,
What everything becomes: Roses open
To worms and dust; this woman, impassioned,
Abandons herself to white ash, black oil,
And doubles death upon herself; I, too,
Am quite unmasked: my naked skull glimmers;
Its grin eases into an earthy leer.
All, all must end: silks and satins moulder,
Radiance palls, philosophies decay.
Property itself gangs up on landlords,
Gathers their bones: worms plough eternity.

REV. F. R. LANGFORD'S MIRACLE

Lightning scratches the oily sky with fire,
Trembles, troubles, the dark white church; apple
Blossoms sag; lumberyard falls mute. Icy
Rain strikes; snow-robed Baptists cringe, cry, scrabble
With soaked hymns, down the quagmired logging trail.
But Reverend Langford faces the storm
And, cyclone-muscular, pine-tall, plunges,
Forces his fierce horse through wet violence.

    Back to that conjurer, Eely, who nursed
With snakes, Langford surges, moors the pitching
Horse at the black cabin, squelches through muck,
And yells for strength to part a kept darkness.
Eely hisses; rain freely floods his cave.
Yelling God words, Langford rips a curtain,
The sun leaps forth. And eyes pleasure to see
The rain becalmed in wine bottles and wells.

DISCOVERY

The text is open.

There was a shining in the bushes
by the river, then I felt her.

Liana, Liana!

She is the Word, a code I read,
fingers caressing the braille she keeps
opening for my touch.

The river is archetypal, is deep;
her swank hair is a river.

I study her and sight African
violets, cassava, wild cherries.

Her true name is Oshun.
Or *Ocean*.

The text is open.

REVELATION

We turn to love before turning to dust so that the grave will
not compress our lives entirely to insects, humus, ash.

Love is our single resistance against the dictatorship of death.

And for the moment of its incarnation, we will worship God,
we will make ourselves beautiful in the glinting of an eye.

EVERYTHING IS FREE

Wipe away tears,
Set free your fears:
Everything is free.
Only the lonely
Need much money:
Everything is free.

   Don't try to bind
The love you find:
Everyone is free.
Your lover's yours —
Surrender force:
Everyone is free.

   The sun melts down,
Spreads gold around:
Everything is free.
The rain is spent
Lending flowers scent:
Everything is free.

   The love you live,
The life you give:
Everything is free.

CLOSE TO HOME

Black train cry, black train wail;
It don't matter,
I'm close to home.
Highway howl in rain and gale;
It don't matter,
I'm close to home.

Child stray, child cry;
Prod'gal kin
Wind up alone.
Gotta say good-bye,
My one true friend:
I'm close to home.

Mother weep, mother wait;
Doncha worry:
God bless them that got their own.
Ope' the pearly gates
And please hurry:
I'm close to home.

VII

The Adoration of Shelley

*My beloved is gone down into his garden,
to the beds of spices, to feed in the garden,
and to gather lilies.*

— *SONG OF SOLOMON* 6:2

THE ARGUMENT

Sun up. Ten months have passed. All things must pass. Snow vanishes into sudden, fresh green. There is everything to be done. Shelley dresses and goes downstairs to prepare the garden. *There is a time to mourn and a time to cease from mourning.*

She moves through new grass, the bright, cool dew drenching her white cotton socks. Shelley rifles the deep pockets of her white peasant dress, finds the packets of seeds she hoarded all winter. It is *Nisan* 1, the first day of April. She steps to the garden, a patch of earth reddened and enriched by rusted metal and rotted wood. The earth smells of history, the new becoming old, the old becoming new. Using strings and four sticks, Shelley plots a miniature orchard of apple, plum, peach, cherry, and apricot trees. Then, poking sequential holes into the ground with a fifth stick, she plants Swiss pansies, sweet peas, carpet-of-snow alyssum, Iceland poppies, sunflowers, mardi gras snapdragons, dwarf jewel nasturtiums, calypso portulaca, squash, marigolds, mayflowers, leaf lettuce, cabbage, and carrots. Thus, she welcomes bees. *Aprill is the most beautiful month.*

X, self-exiled to States County, does not see any of this Beauty. However, he remembers that Shelley's bones are fire and her skin the savoury colour of crushed berries and cream and her scent a sweetness like earth, thistle and hazelnut. He dreams, "Rum and coke, Scotch and a little water, my sweet raven, my love." He can almost hear her voice, a sultry hoarseness. He recalls Shelley: *There was a woman, beautiful as morning.*

EARLY SPRING

. . . snow on green branches —
April has come at last.
The earth is astonished,
maddened, by chlorophyll.
Purple and yellow crocuses
arc through snow:
watercolours rainbow
across white paper.
How beautiful!
We are dressed in flowers
when we wend hither,
when we twine,
and when we ravel hence.
How beatific!
Fulfillment springs
from the roots.

The jar jetting of lilies
atomizes to perfume.
White snow on green branches —
April has come at last.

SELECTED PROVERBS

If you wanna be a well child, have some sense. Hear me
talkin' to you. Can't do no harm to let some words percolate
in your love-heated head. Talkin' 'bout love, learn these facts:

> *Better two lovers in bed than two hypocrites in church.*
> *Better two lovers than none.*

Remember: Love's slaves have young faces on old bodies.
Where there's no faith, there's no love. Pretty is as pretty
does. A rotten man never tells his mind. A wise woman
values her fists. The shack ruined by love is worth more than
the mansion gilt with greed. Anger saves love.

 If love ain't a problem, you're too lucky. But even if your
bed is steady, your house can still shake. Make sure iron love
don't turn to clay. Know this gospel:

> *Indifference signals approval.*
> *Beside a rosebush, dung smells sweet.*

Raise up children like any wondrous creation. Know they are themselves, not you. Learn 'em straightness: the world's a rimracked, slanty place. Think on these truths:

The breast-nursed child howls at oppression.
The bean-fed child darkens early.
The orange moon-born child will wander.
The child's first cry is the first song.

Beware of people with empty hands, big stomachs, and big mouths: They're politicians. In filthy times, they spring up like mushrooms. When the water's low, the fish will be big. Vote for Tories, vote for trouble. Never dig a hole you can't fill. Remember: The road to Hell is paved before elections.

Never mind death. Nothing ever ends. Truth never ages, wisdom never goes out of date, and love never goes out of style. Faith holds the apple to the tree; faith lets the apple fall. Don't allow your feet to lead your heart astray.

— *Cora*

IN STATES COUNTY

In States County, children redeem language:
"Love" is spelled with plucked, twisted daffodils;
"Death" is spelled with rough, wood x's that sign
Its transcendence. "Hate" cannot be pronounced.
When these children, gold-faced and giggling, speak —
It is with the oratory of bees
And the cadence of jays and the joyous
Patois of water raucous over rocks.

    In States County, children roam, naked, new,
At liberty, with a native grammar,
Reading the black crow words in poems of fog,
Speaking the alphabet sounds of crickets,
Singing Eden's lost, original tongue;
Thus, they define no soul as enemy.

TO X

Dear X:

Ma's stewing turnip, cabbage, carrots, cat-tail roots, and chicken in a delicious pot. Pablo's stomping out some song. Am's trying to duet but his tenor's too strong.

Thanks for the poems you mailed me last April — and the rose blossoms. Their fragrance reminded me of China ink.

I've just written you a poem. I hope you like it:

> *The river's beauty*
> *glints*
>
> *and is lost*
>
> *yet remains*
> *beautiful.*

Maybe we just need the right words. We must think the same, trying to get them out to each other. (Smile.)

Understand that I'm slow to love. Too many hurt. Life's too full of all of these such things.

Love,

Shelley

As always and always will be.

IN JARVIS COUNTY

I am lonesome for Spanish — a word! —
And sunflowers sunflowers sunflowers,
The blue moan of gypsy guitar,
The river swafting upon stones,
In Jarvis County.

I am lonesome, too, for a love,
Independent in *passementerie*,
A radical beauty as black
As the moon drowned in the river
In Jarvis County.

I'm coming home, I'm coming home,
Lonesome for Spanish and sunflowers
And a love as complex and black
As water poppling upon stones
In Jarvis County.

THE FIRST DAY OF DESIRE

It's the seventh day of *Nisan*. Stars — fragile milkweed — scatter across southwestern Nova Scotia if anyone bothers them with a stray, languid hand or careless breath of song.

In Shelley's home, bananas — lean, yellow *manna* — scroll upon the table, green vines trail along leafy walls. Black parrots glint overhead, dive to snatch any shining trinket. I slosh through her livingroom that carries the sea smell of the Sixhiboux River and sink into the clover patch armchair.

Because it is a new day, Pablo, Kalamazoo guitar in hand, straggles in and treats us to the spectacle of the constant return of his crescent moon hand to the strings — a trapped trout thrashing, silver, in a net. No wonder we think the moon thrashes in the Sixhiboux. Pablo nods and rhymes:

> *Only once do we love:*
> *Never is there another.*
> *After the first love,*
> *There is no other.*

I came here to Milkland, Honey Country, Beauty Town,

to drown in a baptism of fulfillment. But, Shelley seems to vanish, taking with her all promises of the holiest honey.

I stray outside, bumble around a geyser of raspberries that erupts crooked from black soil. Here, flowers nursed under stained-glass bear dazzling golds, crimsons, and indigos upon their leaves.

*

I seek sombre moonlight but fall into the spill and plunge of grass, while Pablo swaddles the lace and bone of his *fela-mengu* guitar in the white cotton folds of his chest, and breathes life into it with the oxygen of touch. Night blackens with the concentration of bass blue notes.

Repenting of my apostasy, I lurch to my feet, fumble. But someone catches me. Before I can turn around, two small, soft hands cover my eyes from behind and I smell the aroma of bergamot and peach. Then, a soft voice murmurs, "Sing me a rural song, rural song, a sweet, especial rural song."

WILD APPLE TEA

Pablo uncoils in the Cherrybrook chair,
Its legs and back knit by coathanger wire.
He peels a fresh newspaper. There's green wood
Still pressed in the newsprint. He snorts, "Eely
Put Rojane through a second-storey window!
Does that make any sense?" Shelley just grins
And fixes tea, pancakes with apple sauce.
Into the kitchen, Cora sways, murmuring
Macintosh, Granny Smith, Courtland, other
Apples. Sunlight kindles her kindly face.
A vase painted with roses grasps roses
That some romantic's telegraphed Selah.
Pablo readies an arsenal of smokes
As Pushkin goes to operate on cars.

   I awake under a diamond quilt of roses,
And ogle at oceanic wallpaper, blue,
With pink seashells, then blunder into words,
Memories of a broken Kent guitar,
Its single string of silk and steel, and tea
Distilled from orange peel, lemon peel, rosehips,
Hibiscus flowers, cinnamon, peppermint,

And wild apple. *Sweet apple tea!* Shelley
Softens the coffee with Carnation milk.
I hand her apple blossoms of haiku.
Pablo pours out ripe apple wine until
All see seashells, roses, Rojane arcing
To print, and poems sprouting apple blossoms.
O! Steep, steep this poem in apple blossoms!

RADIANT BEING

April, sweet April! I'm in the backwoods watching the last
snow, spying for shoots and buds. Pablo's teaching me
liqueur literacy, the ABCs of Amaretto, Bénédictine (*liquor
antiquorum monachorum bénédictinorum. D.O.M.*), Cointreau,
etc., a rainbow of tastes, smells, feelings. He preaches that life
began with liqueurs distilled from herbs (marjoram and
melissa), bark (cinnamon and pine), roots (celery and
rhubarb), flowers (rose and sunflower), fruit (apples and
blackberries), and aya (what some of us call sugar). Pablo's
the genius of Kahlùa. "God invented liqueurs to help us live
despite evil."

A train lolls. Black ink scuttles across the page. Shelley, I
pray, *ma cherie, mon amoureuse,* that you'll accept my lines all
ending in trochees, my dark verse, my "Song of Acadia":

> *A genius with a guitar*
> *In a vision once I saw:*
> *It was a Nova Scotian lass*
> *Who, against strings, pressed glass,*
> *Chanting of Mount Eulah.*

But, here you come anyway, image of *Germinal* and
Floréal, fresh from your bath, complaining, "My hair's gone
back home because of the water! I don't have good hair!"
But, you do, Shelley! Rubbing in her coconut oil, lanolin,
bergamot, and pure white beeswax pomade, Amarantha
combs your luxury until it glistens. Haloed with baby's
breath, your hair holds the warm scent of earth. In fact,
acushla, you should be laved in flower liqueur because your
Old English name means "from the meadow on the ledge."
Everything is brilliant with meaning. *Those who have eyes, let
them see!* I'm so sick with interest,

> *So sick with daisies, mayflowers, and bluebells,*
> *Shelley, Shelley, Shelley, Shelley, Shelley,*
> *There's nothing I can do but chant my love,*
> *African Baptist beauty, quart'ly queen,*
> *And bring you baskets of the beautiful —*
> *Sweet apple blossoms from an apple grove!*

The poem falls into the abyss of its imprint; the song, into
the cavity of its utterance. Hear blue-gummed Chaucer:

> *. . . Aprill with his shoures soote*
> *The droghte of March hath perced to the roote*
> *And bathed every veyne in swich licour*
> *Of which vertu engendred is the flour . . .*

175

So what if you drop the final 'g' in 'ing' and use the affirmative 'be' as essence? Literature be the tongue you do your lovin' in.

LULLABY

The moon twangs its silver strings;
The river swoons into town;
The wind beds down in the pines,
Covers itself with stars.

ABSOLUTION

X, we are responsible
for Beauty. Miss Dove
coos in the wilderness.
Mister Crow replies.
We were born of the stars
that fell on Nova Scotia.
Nova Scotia! Nova Scotia!
Our country is more than poverty grass,
our lives are more than yellow and white earth.
I'm dreaming of cherries, in July,
plentiful and free to all.

    Lightning blackens the spring
sky. Each darkling sickle of denial
signifies . . . What? Carman observes,
"Some ruin in the April world." Roberts
says, "Sharp drives the rain." I sing:

    Rain wrecks snow,
    wreaks flowers,
    havocs the river.

Every word, every word,
is a lie. But sometimes the lie
tells the truth.

I have studied your numbers,
their ecstacy that mirrors
Cane, the *Cantos*, and the *Canticles*.
I have prepared dark, sweet fruits —
blackberries, raspberries, plums.
Your skin is dark sand or ochre.
Your eyes are black as the Sixhiboux.
The rainwater trembling in the tub
is brimming rose petals.
My words shy, my words shy
into this last, majestic commencement . . .

Let us rise and go to Grand Pré
and loll beneath apple blossoms
and cantillate Longfellow's ballad
about exiled Évangéline,
the pastured scene of her mourning
spread out lushly before our gaze.

X, we are responsible
for Beauty.

ORANGE MOON

Under the orange moon
of Whylah Falls,
Missy addles her guitar
as if she stirs a river.
Shelley descends Mount Eulah
and breaks some apple blossoms.
Every act must reveal Beauty.
Hence, under the orange moon
of Whylah Falls,
I am plucking this poem.

ENVOY

X and I ramble in the wet
To return home, smelling of rain.

We understand death and life now —
How Beauty honeys bitter pain.

VIII

The Apocrypha

Beauty cannot exist outside of humanity.

— SANCHEZ VAZQUEZ

APOLOGY

Stolen from the plots of quixotic Pierrot *and troubled Muddy Waters, these elegiac flowers flourish independently. Irrigated by liquor and tears and dessicated by blistering blues, they bloom in direct moonlight.*

THE PLOT, or NOFASKOSHA

He cries of rivers, stars, moons, and pines,
Saltwater sorrow that descants in lines,
The *Long March* from Jarvis to Whylah Falls,
A shotgunned man dissolving into petals,
His trialled mother who witnesses in cries
Over his corpse cankered white by lilies,
The history of love that could not be,
Though every lyric sketches liberty.

    — *Narrator*

BLACKBERRY BLUES

Blackberry, blackberry, on the vine,
Sweet, bittersweet, blackberry wine,
When will you be mine, all mine?
When will you be mine.

They day comes soft, suggestible, our pines
Are ripe with eloquence, rumours of wings,
While milk and honey burns in the fields,
While milk and honey burns in the fields.

—X

STATUE MAN

A man likes to act a statue —
Bronzen, cold and hefting a sword.
But a woman knows what is true:
He's a boy, easily injured.

— *Cora*

SPRING

Langford erects a scarecrow 'top his roof
To shoo gulls from his drying smelts and fruit.
L'il Toof, cola-coloured, scrounges a man —
Makes him melt like Popsicle in her hands.
Home after six suns, Liana scats blues,
Mumbles Nashville dirges while milkweed snows.
Slick Eely, his feet kicked up like a goat's,
Reels with a bottle of chilled, Tory votes.

 Selah, magnificat in gold and black,
Presses night to stop my train in her tracks.
Gravity thirsts for dew, we thirst for us,
Tasting *Life* in two bright tumblers of Scotch
By the Sixhiboux, where Langford smelts, brings
Everything we ever wanted, everything.

 — X

DAISIES

A storm of daisies dizzies me because
so-and-so says so; yellow weeds or flowers
blow into my face and hands after
the big drunk; the wind pushes flowers
and grass and dirt into my face
and hands; I almost fall
into uprightness; instead, I face
a wall of grass, my feet resting on air,
my toes pressing into the gale of daisies,
my hands clutching at slippery grass.

— *Selah*

189

SHE DISCOVERS HER VOICE

Against the grey wallpaper of that house,
The monotony of beige dawns and dusks,
The cankered roses in the plastic vase,
Her husbands dull, monosyllabic hate,
She hoarded words borrowed from the Bible,
Country tunes, and gross, indifferent children.

   Between her servings of watery tea
And his helpings of woman on woman —
Whelping so many bastards he lost count —
She counted in her secret verse, hidden
In the old scribbler in a drab suitcase
In a drab closet under the old clothes.
When, at last, his secret, hidden cancer
Overthrew him, taking possession,
And she had folded him — beige suit — into
A grey casket, she salvaged her lost poems
And she sang and she sang. Oh, how she sang!

    — Shelley

SHOULD I DIE

Should I die like lightning-stricken pines
Or fall to April's fatal snows,
I'd perish happy if your lips wet mine,
With love as glistening as salves,
With love as glistening as salves.

— *Amarantha*

SONGS OF SOLOMON

Yea, thou art black
but comely —
like the Sixhiboux River,
like Mount Eulah's pines.

I have compared thee,
O my love,
to soft, black night
and raisins and sweet wine.

Behold thou are perfect,
yea, excellent:
thou hast raven's hair;
also, our bed is pine.

— *Pablo*

CANCION ACADIENSE

The moon is an orange sigh,
A blue wind of desire.
Ah, sweet Amarantha,
Life is not forever.

Your eyes are dark roses
In a bouquet of silk.
Look, three or four poets
Tune guitars to your looks.

Death will come no matter
How much I call you "sweet."
But still I call you "sweet,"
Sweet, sweet Amarantha.

— *Pablo*

BAM ON YOUR DOOR

I come and bam on your door,
Crack a keg of homemade nails.
You shake your drawers in my face
Until each bone in me howls.

Let's not smudge this thing over,
Or pretend it's all jes' roses.
I'm drownin' in your river,
I'm carryin' all your crosses.

Damn me or bless me. I'll laugh.
I'm not afraid to love or hate.
If I gotta strike a blow,
I'll hit as boldly as the preachers say.

— *Othello*

DOWN IN THE FLOOD

The frankness of water when you plough
into it, churning a sudden womb
or grave. It clasps you so tightly,
you can't breathe — as if choked
by a deluge of flowers. Watch it
screw and screw and screw.

    The riverbed is charged
with water — liquid lightning.
It churls in its throat
of stone, wanting to bust
the wooden teeth of the dam,
which wants to give,
which wants so much to surrender,
to see how far the water will go —
all that rain-driven rage,
all those tears.

        — Liana

LAMENT

The snow-dissolving crocus,
The butterfly-trembled grass,
Don't seem to think about Death.
But nothing that breathes can last.

Thello, you were night's fleshed-out fire;
You were dawn's star-drizzling frost.
No poet could tell your beauty.
Now, darling, all Beauty's lost.

— *Cora*

THE FUNERAL

The highway blunts itself on stones;
The wind beats bushes senseless;
The river blunders over stones;
A killer calmly buries grass.

    —X

SUICIDE NOTE

There's only Death
And shudders of the eyes.
I stand before the mirror
And become the mirror.

Bye.

— *Scratch*

TAUNT'S HILL

for Chester Jarvis

T. hooks his bass, slits it open; wet notes
Spill out like guts, bloodying night with blues.
He moans over almond-tinctured Leafy,
Wonders when she'll, if she'll . . . then breaks for rum,
Hollers out for "mo' molasses lasses,"
Then keens a black saltwater elegy
For O., whose stomach drained into gravel
After the worming discharge burrowed home,
And the attorney-general, white liar,
Crawled into the papers and laughed like that,
Letting the assassin piss on O.'s bones.

I remember T. like a smile, that thin
Poet of Alcoholics Anonymous,
Who fretted over Ang in the N.S.,
Back when my engine hurt, coughing up weeds,
And Haney's grassfire went loco, turning
His three-generation, pinewood home to snakes.
Queen Anne's lace fans over the foundations.

Last April, nigh spring, T. fell in his chair
While snow heaved and heaved against his window;
He remembered the dead among their corn.
Rum blazed while temperatures went arctic,
Chopped wood faltered in his stove. A blizzard
Hacked an icy path through his brain:
He was climbing Taunt's Hill — at last.

    —X

A POEM WITH THE SINGLE TITLE OF "DESIRE"

You salt away my green, tender letters
To cure — or decay — in forgetfulness.
There, foxed by tears, the dark sheen of words
Will fade slowly to blurs, my Negro blush
Of eloquence corrode to white silence.
Starved for air, my love'll poems coarsen, stiffen
Into stark, crude, Anglo-Saxon stresses
That'll hinder, screw, all pronunciation.

Shelley, how'll your beauty appreciate
If left unsung?

I'll wrench poems from branches,
Scribble your name in the waterfall's noise,
And make all Nature our rose-embroidered
Canticles, to give this dark-complected love
A hearing.

Them that have ears, they will hear.

— X

TO X

X:

Lilac smells of dusk make me smile. Isn't it funny how
Nature keeps her ways no matter how mixed-up our feelings?

In your letter, you thought I'd "run off from you."
I didn't. I saw you come through the door and I was not
even ready for you, dressed in my everyday brown corduroy
and all.

And I'm never sure what to say. My pencil talks better
than my mouth.

Why did you tramp in pitch blackness to Beulah Beach
after whispering, "I love you"? I didn't say it back: Love's no
trifle. But you could have stayed.

I want to see you smile soon. Yes.

I'm waiting impatiently for your love
To come through to me.

Love,
Shelley

The depictions of musical performances incorporate tints suggested by *The New Grove Gospel, Blues and Jazz* (New York: W. W. Norton & Company, 1986). *The Poetry of the Blues* (New York: Oak Publications, 1963), by Samuel Charters, offered a palette of signs. Ezra Pound's translation of a Li Po poem shadows "The River Pilgrim: A Letter," while lines by Federico Garcia Lorca, translated by Stephen Spender and J. L. Gili, colour "In Acadian Jarvis County." *The Second South Shore Phrase Book* (Hantsport: Lancelot Press, 1985), edited by Lewis J. Poteet, and *Black English* (New York: Random House, 1972), by J. L. Dillard, accented some speeches. *The Scofield Reference Bible*, edited by C. I. Scofield, yielded background tones. I have worried these originals into original worries.

The publisher is grateful for the permission to reprint the following photographs: cover, pages 16, 41, 157, 158, 160, 176 & 186 (Georgia Cunningham Collection, Public Archives of Nova Scotia); page 65 (Paul Yates Collection, Public Archives of Nova Scotia); page 97 (W. H. Buckley, Public Archives of Nova Scotia); pages iv, v & xxxiii ("Waterfalls," 1931, Albert Van, National Archives); page 2 (R. W. Brock, National Archives); pages 32 ("The Toilers," 1933) & 46 ("Through the Mist," 1932, Clifford M. Johnston, National Archives); pages 98, 100 & 124 (Victor-Gabriel Brodeur, Department of National Defence, National Archives); pages 72, 74, 119 & 132 (National Archives); pages 130 & 135 (Author's Archives); and pages 141, 182 & 184 (Author).

About the Author

The son of William and Geraldine Clarke, George Elliott Clarke was born in Windsor, Nova Scotia in 1960. A graduate of the University of Waterloo, Dalhousie University and Queen's University, he now teaches Canadian and African Diasporic Literature at the University of Toronto. He has also worked as an editor, publisher, social worker, researcher, journalist and parliamentary aide. His other books of poetry are *Saltwater Spirituals and Deeper Blues* (Pottersfield, 1983), *Lush Dreams, Blue Exile* (Pottersfield, 1994) and *Beatrice Chancy* (Polestar, 1999). The original edition of *Whylah Falls* received the Archibald Lampman Award for Poetry in 1991. It has been staged as a play (in 1997, 1998 and 2000), produced as a radio play (in 1996) and published in a stage version by Playwrights Canada Press (in 1999). *Whylah Falls* was begun in Halifax in 1986 and completed in Ottawa, where Clarke lived from 1987 to 1991.

Whylah Falls was designed by Val Speidel

in 11 point Cloister Old Style on 17 point leading.

Cloister Old Style was designed in the United States

by Morris Benton on the model of Jenson's Roman,

and is issued in digital form by Monotype.

At Raincoast Books we are committed to protecting the

environment and to the responsible use of natural resources.

We are acting on this commitment by working with suppliers

and printers to phase out our use of paper produced from

ancient forests — this book is one step towards that goal.

It is printed on 100% ancient-forest-free paper (100% post-

consumer recycled), processed chlorine- and acid-free, and

supplied by New Leaf Paper; it is printed with vegetable-based

inks by Houghton Boston Printers in Saskatoon, Saskatchewan.

POETRY *from* POLESTAR

Polestar takes pride in creating books that enrich our understanding of the world, and in introducing discriminating readers to exciting writers. These independent voices illuminate our history, stretch the imagination and engage our sympathies.

Beatrice Chancy · by George Elliott Clarke
This brilliant dramatic poem is the first literary work to treat the issue of Canadian slavery. "Clarke . . . carries this story from our heads to our hearts to that gut feeling we all get when we have heard a devastating truth." — NIKKI GIOVANNI
1-896095-94-1 · $16.95 CAN/$14.95 USA

Blue · by George Elliott Clarke
Blue is black, profane, surly, damning, and unrelenting in its brilliance. George Elliott Clarke has written urgent and necessary poems about the experience of being black in North America.
1-55192-414-5 · $19.95 CAN/$12.95 USA

Constellations: Twenty Years of Stellar Poetry from Polestar
Including works by Kate Braid, George Elliott Clarke, Paulette Jiles, John MacKenzie, Nadine McInnis, Shani Mootoo, Pat Lowther, Gregory Scofield and others.
1-55192-500-1 · $18.95 CAN/$12.95 USA

I Knew Two Metis Women · by Gregory Scofield
Stunning in their range and honesty, these poems about Scofield's mother and aunt are a rich, multi-voiced tribute to a generation of First Nations people.
1-896095-96-8 · $16.95 CAN/$12.95 USA

Into the Early Hours · by Aislinn Hunter
"The poems in this debut collection are so rich and deft that they leave you breathless. I'm telling everyone I know to buy this book, to read it into the early hours and long after." — LORNA CROZIER
1-55192-498-6 · $18.95 CAN/$12.95 USA

Inward to the Bones: Georgia O'Keeffe's Journey with Emily Carr · by Kate Braid
In 1930, Emily Carr met Georgia O'Keeffe at an exhibition in New York. Inspired by this meeting, poet Kate Braid describes what might have happened afterwards.
1-896095-40-2 · $16.95 CAN/$12.95 USA

Sledgehammer · by John MacKenzie
This stunning, eloquent debut is a vibrant meditation on love and loss, tradition and invention, community and the individual.
1-896095-56-9 · $16.95 CAN/$12.95 USA